I0594044

Passion Restored

Special Editoin

Gallagher Brothers

Carrie Ann Ryan

Passion Restored
A Gallagher Brothers Novel
By: Carrie Ann Ryan
© 2017 Carrie Ann Ryan
Cover Art by Sweet N Spicy Designs

Praise for Carrie Ann Ryan....

"Count on Carrie Ann Ryan for emotional, sexy, character driven stories that capture your heart!" – Carly Phillips, NY Times bestselling author

"Carrie Ann Ryan's romances are my newest addiction! The emotion in her books captures me from the very beginning. The hope and healing hold me close until the end. These love stories will simply sweep you away." ∼ NYT Bestselling Author Deveny Perry

"Carrie Ann Ryan writes the perfect balance of sweet and heat ensuring every story feeds the soul." - Audrey Carlan, #1 New York Times Bestselling Author

"Carrie Ann Ryan never fails to draw readers in with passion, raw sensuality, and characters that pop off the page. Any book by Carrie Ann is an absolute treat." – New York Times Bestselling Author J. Kenner

"Carrie Ann Ryan knows how to pull your heart-strings and make your pulse pound! Her wonderful Redwood Pack series will draw you in and keep you reading long into the night. I can't wait to see what comes next with the new generation, the Talons. Keep them coming, Carrie Ann!" –Lara Adrian, New York Times bestselling author of CRAVE THE NIGHT

"With snarky humor, sizzling love scenes, and brilliant, imaginative worldbuilding, The Dante's Circle series reads as if Carrie Ann Ryan peeked at my personal wish list!" – NYT Bestselling Author, Larissa Ione

"Carrie Ann Ryan writes sexy shifters in a world full of passionate happily-ever-afters." – *New York Times* Bestselling Author Vivian Arend

"Carrie Ann's books are sexy with characters you can't help but love from page one. They are heat and heart blended to perfection." *New York Times* Bestselling Author Jayne Rylon

Carrie Ann Ryan's books are wickedly funny and deliciously hot, with plenty of twists to keep you guessing. They'll keep you up all night!" USA Today Bestselling Author Cari Quinn

"Once again, Carrie Ann Ryan knocks the Dante's Circle series out of the park. The queen of hot, sexy, enthralling paranormal romance, Carrie Ann is an author not to miss!" *New York Times* bestselling Author Marie Harte

Dedication

For Liz, who asked if I could write about a stacked, hourglass, blue-eyed, and adorable blonde woman named Liz whose hero loves oral.
This one's for you.

Acknowledgments

Passion Restored was one of those books that came together with the help of so many. I know I couldn't have done it without Team Carrie Ann! So thank you Charity, Chelle, and Tara! You guys support me so much and I love you guys for it!

Thank you to Chris, Jenn, Lynda, and the others in LA at the photo shoot who helped me with this photo shoot. You guys rocked this cover out of the part and Chris is TOTALLY Owen.

And a giant thank you to Kennedy and Dr. Hubby for pulling me through when I had to work long nights to get this book finished!

As always, I couldn't be here without my readers, so thank you for reading each of my books and thank you once more for taking a chance with the Gallagher Brothers.

Happy reading!

~Carrie Ann

Passion Restored

Owen Gallagher fell in lust at first sight with Liz McKinley on the dance floor.

But in the next blink, she was gone and his life changed forever.

When an accident forces him to step back from the world he knows and actually rest for the first time in his life, he's no longer the carefree guy his friends and family know.

He's grumpy, cantankerous, and doesn't want to be nursed back to health.

That is, until he realizes Liz is not only the one who can help him—but happens to be his new neighbor.

Liz doesn't want to take a chance on the sexy man next door. She's had enough heartache and pain in her life. But Owen changes something in her she'd wanted to keep hidden.

And now the two of them have a chance at something no one saw coming...as long as the two of them can handle the heat.

Chapter One

There was just something about a woman in jeans. In fact, he had a particular pair of jeans on his mind. They were deliciously tight and molded to this woman's body so perfectly that Owen Gallagher had to grip the edge of the bar so he didn't fall to his knees in thanks. It wasn't every day that a woman left him breathless by merely walking into a building. Owen swallowed hard, thanking God once again for tight jeans and the way a woman could *move*.

His younger brother, Murphy, raised an eyebrow at him before turning so he could follow Owen's line of sight. Owen knew when Murphy had spotted her because the younger man whistled low through his teeth before he turned over his shoulder and tilted the neck of his beer.

"Nice," Murphy mouthed as he turned back so he was standing side to side with Owen. This way both of them had a clear line of sight but could also talk to each other like they'd been doing before the woman in jeans showed up.

Owen swallowed hard, his mind going to dirty places better left untraveled. "Nice" wasn't a good enough word to describe this particular siren in blue jeans. The woman was all curves and sex appeal, even if she hadn't exactly dressed the part of a bar goer. In fact, when she'd stormed into the bar just a few moments prior, Owen hadn't missed the apprehension in her gaze before it turned to annoyance.

She'd scanned the space before stomping toward a group of men and a single woman in the corner. Owen hadn't really paid attention to that group other than noticing them in passing and still wasn't looking too hard. He only had eyes for the sexy, blonde woman in a decently loose shirt and tight jeans.

Even though her shirt wasn't clingy, he could still tell that she was pretty damn stacked and would have more than enough to fill his hands. He loved when that happened. Loved putting his face between a woman's breasts and sucking and licking until she came. He adored watching the way her tits swayed back and forth when he fucked her from behind, and how they bounced high when she rode him, her hands sliding down his thighs as she arched her back.

Of course, with breasts that perfect, he'd have to rise so he could lick them, suck them, and even bite down on her nipples. Then he'd cup her with both hands, rolling the tight nubs between his fingers as she continued to ride him like he was a damn pony.

It wasn't just the blonde's breasts that held his attention, however. The sway of her hips called to him, too, beckoned him closer with each step. She had a perfect set of curves and a delightfully lush ass that just begged to be fucked. He knew the curves of her butt would jiggle and shake when he fucked her, and he'd have more than enough to hold onto as he pounded into her. And those hips? Hell, those hips were the perfect handles, no matter the position the two of them took as they fucked until the sun came up.

His cock hardened painfully behind his zipper, and he let out a groan. Well, shit. He hadn't fantasized like that about a woman he hadn't even spoken to in a long while. Maybe Murphy was right, and he needed to get laid.

He'd turned into a damn lecher and he didn't like it one bit.

Annoyed with himself, Owen sipped his club soda nice and slow so he didn't choke on his tongue, and so he'd have something to do with his hands now that he'd let go of the damn bar.

The blonde woman spoke to another gorgeous, brown-haired woman, pulling her away from the men in the corner. The guys didn't seem too pleased about that, but they didn't crowd the women either. Owen counted that as a blessing, and before he did something stupid like drool over this unnamed blonde, he pulled his attention from her and shifted it to his brother.

The same brother who now stared at the two women with an equally hungry look in his eyes.

Well, shit.

"I'm not going to call dibs since we aren't in high school and have grown beyond that, but..." Owen trailed off when Murphy chuckled.

"Yeah, no dibs necessary. I'm pretty sure your stare like a puppy that just found a delicious new chew toy to chomp and hump in equal measure was for the blonde." Murphy winked. "I've always been partial to brunettes myself."

Owen shook his head, a smile playing on his lips. "Good to know." He took a sip of his soda. "I wasn't that bad, was I?"

Murphy raised a brow and set his half-empty beer down on the bar. They had both driven here tonight and had a one-beer limit, though Owen had opted for club soda since he had a headache.

"You couldn't keep your eyes off her. I'm surprised you didn't follow her around, trying to catch her scent. Plus, your jaw dropped just a little bit, though you somehow kept in the drool. Good for you."

Owen flipped Murphy off before setting his drink down next to his brother's beer. "Shut up. I wasn't close to drooling." He wiped his chin just in case, and Murphy threw his head back and laughed. "See, no drool."

"That's probably not the best way to show you weren't acting like a horny teenager. Been a while, has it?" Murphy grinned, and Owen resisted the urge to punch the other man in the shoulder.

"It hasn't been *that* long." Owen winced as he remembered that he hadn't slept with anyone since Tracy, and that was over three months ago. He and Tracy slept together off and on when their schedules and relationships matched up. Recently, there hadn't been much matching. If he were acting this hard-up for a woman he didn't even know, maybe he needed to call Tracy and see about letting off some steam. Yet even thinking that didn't appeal. Didn't really sound like a good idea at all.

"If you have to qualify it, then it's been too long,"

Murphy explained. "Why don't you go ask her out? Or at least talk to her. What could you lose?"

From the way Blondie glared at her friend, Owen was pretty sure he could lose something like a finger...or worse.

"I'll pass, thanks."

"Suit yourself," Murphy said simply before ordering a soda for himself.

"Not in the mood to finish your beer tonight?" Owen asked.

His brother shook his head. "Have a headache."

Owen's shoulders stiffened. "Are you okay? Should you be sitting?"

Murphy glared. "You had a headache too, ass. Hence why you're not even trying to drink a beer. We had a long day at the jobsite today—as you well know since you were there—and my head hurts. Every single little twinge and ache aren't cause for concern, you know. I've been cancer free for years."

Owen let out a breath and leaned on a stool. "Sorry, Murph. I get overprotective."

Murphy nodded at the male bartender who handed over his drink and sighed at Owen. "I know you do. All three of you do. I've been dealing with three overprotective brothers since the day I was born."

"You'd think you'd get used to it by now," Owen said

with a smile he knew didn't reach his eyes. Murphy had been sick when he was a child. Really sick. And then, when everyone had grown up, and they all thought they were in the clear, Murphy had gotten sick again.

It had taken a toll on their mother, who died a few years back. Their father had gone right along with her a couple of years later. Not that he, Graham, or Jake actually blamed Murphy for their parents' deaths. Their mom's and dad's hearts had given out at a young age for a number of reasons, but Owen knew Murphy blamed himself.

And the fact that every time Murphy got even so much as a sniffle, the remaining Gallagher clan would snap into action and overdo it probably didn't help. Owen couldn't help it, though. He was a fixer. An organizer. And if he could find a way to color-code and label his way to making sure Murphy stayed healthy for the rest of his *very* long life, Owen would do it.

"I'm fine, Owen. Just drop it, okay?"

Owen studied his brother's face, from the hard lines of his jaw to the color in his cheeks, and nodded. No matter what Murphy said or did, Owen would be there to make sure his baby brother was okay. He would never forget how pale Murphy had looked in his hospital bed as a young kid and then later as a teenager.

Never.

"I can drop it," Owen said slowly before shaking off the memories that would haunt him until his dying breath.

"Good."

They lapsed into silence for a few moments while the sound of the bar filled Owen's ears. He liked coming here after long days at work. It was the perfect place when he wasn't quite in the mood to deal with the silence of his empty home but also didn't want the loud music of some of the other bars around the area. Plus, this place was pretty close to where he and the rest of his brothers lived, so it was one of their usual destinations. Of course, none of the four of them were getting any younger, and with two of the four married with children, going out to bars was quickly becoming a thing of the past.

Owen winced as he rubbed his lower back and thought about the day they'd had at the project site. Yeah, he was definitely getting older. He, Murphy, and their eldest brother, Graham, owned and operated Gallagher Brothers Restoration. Jake, his second-eldest brother, helped as well, though he hadn't wanted a stake in the company since he had a business of his own. Graham was the lead contractor, and Murphy the architect. Jake came in for special jobs as the artist, and

Owen...well, Owen organized them all. Sometimes to a fault.

Or at least that's what Murphy had claimed that morning.

"So, do you know what you're going to get Rowan for her birthday?" Murphy asked after a few moments. Rowan was their niece, Graham and Blake's daughter. But since Rowan hadn't been in the brothers' lives until recently, they weren't quite sure what to do when it came to gifts for the little girl.

Owen sighed. "I have no idea what to get a little girl for her birthday. It's not like we grew up with sisters."

Murphy nodded. "True. Maybe Maya and Blake will help us out. And we have a few weeks to get things done." Maya Montgomery-Gallagher had married Jake, as well as another man, Border to complete their triad, but she had been in the Gallaghers' lives for years. Well, she'd legally married Border and had completed a commitment ceremony with Jake since poly marriages weren't exactly legal, but anyone who knew them considered the three married in every way that mattered.

"Maybe," Owen agreed. "But I think they're going to want us to figure things out ourselves."

Murphy snorted. "Well, you're the one who organizes us all and does all the research. Make a list, and I'll pick something."

Owen flipped his little brother off. "I do more than organize lists for you."

"Of course. You get us coffee, too. With our initials on it so we don't drink the wrong one. Not that Graham ever pays attention."

"You're the one who took the 'G' this morning so shut up." A pause. "And I do more than just that. You realize that, right?" He didn't like thinking that his brothers saw him as a glorified admin rather than an integral part of the company. Not that their admins weren't vital. He just thought he was *more*.

Murphy frowned. "Of course. You do way more. I'm just messing with you. You have that new project coming up, and the rest of us didn't have anything to do with that."

Owen studied his drink. "It's not final yet." But it would be. He had a good feeling about it. He'd done all the research, spent countless hours dealing with the man that owned the property and the companies that wanted in on the action... Usually, all of the Gallagher brothers worked together for a new project, but with Graham getting married, Jake having a new baby, and Murphy picking up the slack, Owen had been the one to work on the next phase of their company alone.

He was so fucking nervous, and yet excited all at the same time.

"It will be. You're good at what you do." Murphy looked over Owen's shoulder and grinned. "And it looks like you're going to have a chance to see what I'm really good at." He smiled slowly. "Ladies."

Owen turned as Blondie and her friend walked over to the bar, a frown on Blondie's face and a grin on the brunette's. While the other woman was gorgeous, Owen only had eyes for the blonde.

"Hi, boys," the brunette said with a slight drunken slur. "Liz is making me leave, but I wanted to say hi. I'm Tessa." She held out her hand, looked down, and laughed before pulling her arm back. "Sorry. Not at work. I guess handshakes in bars are weird, right?"

Blondie—*Liz*, he corrected himself—closed her eyes, and he assumed counted to ten. He couldn't help but feel for her right then. Picking up inebriated friends from bars when you were *clearly* not in the mood wasn't the easiest thing in the world.

"We're all friends here," Murphy said softly. "I'm Murphy, this is my brother, Owen."

Owen nodded at them both, though his eyes were still on Liz. "Hey."

"Hey," Liz said with a soft scowl. "Now that we've said hello, Tessa, we're going home. I'm exhausted and not in the mood to deal with bars and the grabby hands of the dudes that frequent them." She winced and looked over at Owen and Murphy. "Sorry. No offense."

Murphy snorted and held up his hands. "No offense taken, *and* no grabby hands here. Nice to meet you both."

Owen tilted his head and studied the shadows beneath Liz's eyes. She may be exhausted, but he had a feeling it wasn't just lack of sleep that gave her that look.

And why did he care?

He'd literally just met her and her friend and had said all of one word so far. He should just let them go and head home himself. He wasn't in the mood for a bar night either it seemed.

"Get some sleep, ladies," Owen said after a moment. "Nice to meet you both."

Tessa pouted but winked as she did it, completely ruining the effect. "Nighty-night, boys."

Liz rolled her eyes, a small smile playing on her lips even as she tried to frown. "Good night." She pulled at Tessa's arm, and the two of them made their way out of the bar, most of the eyes of the men in the building following them. Owen couldn't blame the guys as he was one of them, but he still felt a little bad about it.

A guy tripped his way up to Owen's side and snorted. "Looks good coming and going. I'd fuck either one of them, but that blonde one seems a bit stiff. Maybe she just needs a little D to get over whatever stick is up her ass."

Owen looked over at the idiot and narrowed his eyes. "Watch it," he growled softly. "She was just picking up her friend."

The guy raised a brow. "What the fuck ever. She needs to get over herself."

The asshole's friend cupped himself, rocking into his hand. "She just needs to be stuffed with something other than that stick."

Murphy put his hand on Owen's shoulder, and that's when Owen realized he'd moved forward ever so slightly toward the other two men. And now that Owen got a good look at them, he recognized them as the group Tessa had been talking to before in the corner.

Owen might have had fantasies about Liz—and now felt like an asshole about them—but in the daydreams, she'd been a willing participant, not something to fuck and get over like these guys insinuated. And hell, he was glad Liz had gotten Tessa out of there because a woman drinking alone with these guys would only lead to bad things.

Fucking idiots.

"Let's go," Owen growled. "I'm done."

Murphy squeezed his shoulder and pulled him back again. "I'm with you."

The other guys ignored them, going back to whatever crude and mundane conversation they'd been having before, and Owen was grateful for it. He didn't want to get in a fight tonight. Didn't want to deal with the inevitable injuries to his hands—even though he and Murphy would have won for sure against these drunk idiots—and, hell, he definitely didn't want to deal with the cops.

Liz and Tessa hadn't asked for their help and weren't even there any longer, but Owen still had the desire to teach the guys a lesson.

And because there was nothing he could do other than show them how to treat women, he slung back the rest of his club soda so he had a bit of pep thanks to the bubbles for the drive home and headed out of the bar with Murphy.

The parking lot wasn't that full since it was the middle of the week, but since he and Murphy had gotten there at different times, they hadn't been able to park next to one another.

"See you in the morning," Owen grumbled.

"Nine, right?" Murphy asked, his eyes too innocent.

"Seven, and you know that." Though Murphy would probably stroll in bleary-eyed and in need of caffeine at seven-fifteen or so. Their little brother was *not* a morning person and usually worked later than all of them to make up for it.

"God, why are there two sevens in the day? I mean, hell, isn't seven in the evening enough for us?" Murphy clutched his chest and took a couple of steps back, and Owen shook his head.

"You'll be fine." And, thankfully, they were calling it an early night tonight since they did, in fact, have a *very* early morning. Owen would probably set out at six or so to pick up something to eat for the crew and coffee for his brothers. They never asked it of him, but he always did it. Anyone could have picked it up, but then Owen wouldn't be able to make sure it was done correctly *and* on time.

So he was a little anal-retentive.

What of it?

He said goodbye to Murphy and headed back to his car, aware that others were filing out of the bar, as well, their voices carrying on the wind. Owen rolled his head on his shoulders and stuffed his hands into his pockets as he crossed the long lot to where he'd parked under a street lamp.

At the sound of a shout, he turned, the hairs on the back of his neck standing on end. Lights filled his vision, and he took a staggering step back, throwing his hands up to shield his face.

The sound of an engine filled his ears, and he only had a moment to realize what it was he saw until he couldn't see anything else. The truck—it had to be a truck with the size of those lights—clipped him in the side, and Owen flew.

He felt weightless and yet too heavy all at the same time.

His body went numb before it felt as if he'd caught on fire.

He hit the pavement hard enough to crack bones—maybe a few ribs—and he tried to scream, only he couldn't get enough air. His body skidded across the parking lot for far too long, his head scraping the gravel along the way.

Then he stopped.

His body shaking.

His mind whirling.

And yet he couldn't focus.

Couldn't see.

Couldn't breathe.

The sound of tires burning rubber as they skidded away made him want to wince, but he couldn't pull his arms up to cover his face. Rapid footsteps sounded as someone came near and others shouted for help.

But Owen didn't do anything.

He couldn't.

When he finally opened his eyes and saw Murphy above him, his brother's eyes wide, tears running down his pale cheeks, the streetlight hovering above him like a halo, Owen figured this might be the end.

Because no Gallagher looked like an angel, not even his baby brother.

Owen tried to reach out, to say something.

But the darkness came, and then there was nothing.

Nothing.

Chapter Two

"Feel any better?" Liz McKinley asked her friend as she tucked Tessa in bed. They'd only been home a few minutes, and Tessa had decided to strip down to nothing but her underwear on the way to her bedroom. While she loved her friend, dealing with Drunk Tessa was a pain.

Thankfully, neither of them indulged to this point often.

In fact, Liz couldn't remember the last time she'd indulged like this. That was kind of sad, honestly. But from the miserable look on Tessa's face, Liz was pretty sure neither of them wanted to drink this much ever again. But her friend had had a shit day, and sometimes, drinking oneself into oblivion before calling a friend for help was the only way to get through it.

"Mmph."

Liz snorted at Tessa's response and finished tucking her in. Her friend was down for the count but would wake up the next morning fully functional and without a hangover. It had been that way since they were eighteen and living in the dorms. Liz honestly hated the other woman for the way she bounced back sometimes. Maybe once they hit thirty things would change, but for now, Tessa would probably be better off than Liz once the sun rose.

The two of them had been roommates since college and now owned their first home together. Most people wouldn't go in on home ownership with their best friend, but Liz and Tessa weren't most people. They'd been through hell and some versions of peace together and had come out on top. There wasn't anything Liz wouldn't do for Tessa, and she knew Tessa felt the same about her.

Liz didn't know exactly why Tessa had gone off to the bar alone tonight to drink away her worries. All she knew was that she'd had a bad day. But she knew she'd hear about it eventually. At least, she hoped so. For as open as Tessa claimed to be, her friend kept things tight to her chest.

Though, honestly, Liz was much the same and never claimed to be open. She'd worked a full shift that day and had wanted to come home and start unpacking what was there. They'd moved in the week before, and hadn't had time to do anything except find a pan to cook with and some sheets to sleep on. The other set of movers would be at the house with the rest of their things from storage in a few days, and Liz knew they at least had to make a pathway for the guys to walk through.

With both Liz and Tessa working at the hospital, though, she had a feeling that neither of them would have time for anything personal for a while. Her position in the ER was tenuous at best since the hospital was once again facing cutbacks, and while she was good at what she did, she had a bad feeling about what the numbers told her.

They had a few too many nurses on payroll, though in reality, there could never be enough nurses when it came to triage. Not that anyone in the administrative department other than Tessa understood that. And Tessa couldn't do anything but batten down the hatches in her own position thanks to boardroom politics.

Liz let out a groan as she left Tessa's room and ran her hand through her long, blonde hair that was in desperate need of a trim. She'd been stressing over patients all day, and now she was home stressing about her job. She truly needed a life.

Of course, the image of the dark-haired man with the very sexy and trimmed beard came to mind and she cursed herself. There was *no* way she was going there. Not with that man or his brother.

And though the one who'd called himself Murphy was good-looking, Liz only had eyes for Owen.

And that just pissed her off.

She didn't have time for a man, especially one that spent a weeknight in a bar trolling for women. There were more important things for her to deal with since her job was slowly killing her. She still hadn't unpacked her clothes beyond her scrubs—not that she wore anything but scrubs most days of the week—and she wasn't sure when she'd last had an orgasm.

Liz stopped in her tracks on the way to the kitchen.

Why the *hell* had she tacked on her lack of orgasms to that train of thought? Had it really been that long since she'd had sex? Hell, it had probably been that long since she'd gotten herself off in the shower.

Liz tried to mentally do the math and just got more upset with herself. If she needed more than two hands to calculate the last time she'd come, she should probably be using her hands for something else.

Determined, she rolled her shoulders back and headed to her bedroom, only to curse under her breath as her phone buzzed. She knew that buzz, the two quick bursts before a longer one.

The hospital.

Damn it. She'd already worked her shift and didn't want to go back, but she knew if they called her in, she'd be there. Unlike most of the other men and women in her unit, she didn't have kids or a husband waiting at home. Apparently, that meant her free time wasn't as valuable as others'.

Of course, a little voice inside her head whispered to her that if she had more time off, maybe she'd actually meet a man and get started on making those babies.

Damn how she missed orgasms.

Beautiful, long orgasms that made her all revved up and sated at the same time. There was truly nothing better than a man between her legs as he ate her out. He'd use his tongue and his fingers just right, and she'd come right on his face.

With a sad sigh for dreams long forgotten, she pulled out her phone and answered on the second round of buzzes.

"Liz here."

"We need you in. You didn't work overtime today so you can work a half-shift."

Liz crossed her eyes at the sound of her supervisor, Nancy's, voice. While technically the math of her statement worked out, it still wasn't that feasible. Liz was exhausted and doing an extra shift—partial or no—wouldn't be safe for anyone long-term.

"I can come in, but I don't know about working a full half-shift. You'll have to double check the math so we don't go over."

"You do your job, and I'll worry about the math. Get in, now."

And with that, she hung up, and Liz lifted her lip in a snarl. She loved her job, she really did—except for the times she hated it. She was well and truly on her way to a burnout, and she prayed that no one got singed on her way down.

Lives depended on it.

The ER was packed to the brim by the time she got there, and though it wasn't a full moon, the place had that same kind of energy. Tonight wasn't going to be an easy one that was for sure.

She quickly stored her things in her locker and grabbed a cup of coffee, imagining it was from her maker at home and not the sludge she currently poured into her body. Since this wasn't her shift, she went straight to the board to see where she was needed and what she could do.

The head nurse—Liz's supervisor—Nancy, called her over as soon as Liz got to the central station, and Liz made her way as she finished her drink.

"Where do you need me?" she asked and threw away her cup in the recycling bin under the desk.

"There's an MVA in room seventeen. It looks like the car just clipped him according to the on-scene reports, but he went down hard on the pavement."

Liz's brows went up. "A car hit a pedestrian?"

"Yep. Looks like it might have been deliberate, too, since it was in a parking lot," Nancy put in. The other woman loved gossip but was real clear on the lines of patient confidentially, thankfully.

"I'm on my way," Liz said as she made her way to the room. She grabbed a quick glance at the chart as the others worked and moved to wash her hands and prep before she started.

"Call for the OR," the doctor on call stated. "Looks like a lacerated spleen."

Liz held back a wince. If the man had a lacerated spleen, there was a good chance he'd lose it tonight. And while that wasn't life-threatening if they were quick about their diagnosis, it meant there could be other internal injuries.

When Liz got to the doctor's side, she blinked as she looked down at the patient in the bed.

"Hey, Liz," Owen stated, his voice filled with pain.

How he was awake right then was beyond her. And, holy hell, what a small world. She felt as if he'd just spoken to her at the bar, and now, here he was.

"You know him?" the other nurse, Lisa, asked, a curious gleam in her eyes. Liz did her best to avoid being the butt of gossip around the hospital, and now it looked like Lisa wanted to catch something juicy.

"Mr. Gallagher," Liz said, pointedly ignoring Lisa. "Can you tell me how you're feeling?"

"Like I got hit by a car," Owen said with a cough before trying to hide a wince. *Tough guy*, she thought. But even the toughest of the tough needed pain meds every once in a while.

"Looks like it, too." She took his vitals again, noting that while he had to be in pain, his BP was decent, and he didn't have a high temperature. His heart rate was slightly elevated, but considering what he'd been through, it made sense.

"I guess this is one way to get you to talk to me," Owen said, and Liz wanted to ask him to shut up. She did *not* need the staff thinking she had a thing going on with her patient.

"It would seem. Now, let's get you all fixed up, shall we?" She went back to work as the others did their thing. From the looks of it, Owen had a fractured clavicle, a few broken and bruised ribs, as well as the lacerated spleen that required surgery. And from the way his eyes tracked and the fact that he'd apparently been unconscious at the scene, he more than likely had a minor concussion, as well.

All in all, not too bad, considering he'd had a run-in with a freaking car.

"Will you talk to my brothers?" Owen asked, his words slurring. They'd pumped him full of drugs to dampen the pain and prep him for surgery so it was no wonder he was going under. He should have been out of it long before this.

Brothers? As in more than one?

That was a dangerous thought.

"I'll make sure the doctor lets them know what's going on," she promised.

"You. Make sure it's you," Owen whispered. "They're gonna freak..." And with that, he was out, and Liz was feeling a little confused.

Why on earth did it need to be her? She'd spoken to him quite rudely for all of two minutes earlier, but apparently, that meant something to this man.

Lisa gave her a look that spoke of more than Liz wanted to get into right then, and Dr. Wilder frowned.

"Surgery is taking him up now, but from what I can see, it should just be his spleen. Why don't you come with me to talk to the family?" he asked, his words clipped. Dr. Wilder did *not* like his role usurped, but at the same time, he didn't like talking with families either.

Liz shook her head. "I don't know them, Dr. Wilder."

"The patient seemed to think you do, so you're coming with me." He walked out of the room, and Liz watched as the techs wheeled Owen out of the ER. She knew their surgical unit was the best in Denver, and he was in good hands, but for some reason, she got a little nervous kick in her gut...one she didn't usually get for patients. Ever.

"Better go, Liz," Lisa said from behind her, and Liz turned to face the other woman. "I'll do the final check in here so you can go meet Mr. Gallagher's family. Or maybe you already know them." She fluttered her eyelashes; a smile Liz didn't quite like appearing on her face. With all of them fully aware that someone would probably lose their job soon, Liz couldn't let something as silly as a misunderstanding get blown up.

Liz shook her head as she took off her gown. "I don't know them. I've seen him around town once. That's it." She had to be at least that honest since Owen had known her name, but she wasn't about to let Lisa know she'd met Owen and his brother at a bar with a very drunken Tessa. There only so much she'd share, after all. "You know we don't work on family members or friends, Lisa. I wouldn't do that. Now, if that's all, I need to go meet with Dr. Wilder and the patient's family."

She turned on her heel and left Lisa behind her, smirking like the cat that got the canary. Liz ground her back molars, annoyed that she was the center of attention. Nurses with a shred of gossip to pass along were nothing to mess with, and now that they'd caught something on the wind, they would be hounding her forever. Liz had never been one of the inside clique, always focusing on her job instead of the politics that came with it, but now she was afraid she'd made a mistake by not taking more care with that.

She hurried after Dr. Wilder, aware that Lisa had probably already beelined her way to the nurses' station to talk about how a patient seemed to *know* her and wanted *only* Liz to talk to his family.

Because that wasn't weird at all or anything.

She caught up to Dr. Wilder and matched her pace with his, though his legs were far longer and she was just about running. However, she was a nurse, and this was what she did on a daily basis so it was nothing new.

What *was* new, however, was what had just occurred.

"So, how do you know Mr. Gallagher?" Dr. Wilder

asked. They were almost to the waiting room doors so, thankfully, Liz didn't have long to deal with how to answer.

"I don't," she said honestly.

Dr. Wilder turned his head to her and cocked a brow. "Since he specifically asked you to talk to his family, I'm going to have to disagree with you there."

Liz sighed. Of all the doctors in the ER, she liked Dr. Wilder the best, even if he was the coldest. He was honest about the type of man he was, and she appreciated that. However, that didn't mean she wanted to get into this with him right then.

"I met him and his brother, Murphy, tonight while picking up Tessa." She didn't say where, as that wasn't any of his business. "I spoke maybe four or five words to him before Tessa and I left to go home. I had a long day today, and planned to go to bed before I got called back into work."

She tried not to blush as she thought of what she had *actually* been planning to do before bed. *Way* too much information.

"Seems weird if that's all it was. We aren't exactly a small town."

"I know," she answered honestly. "But that's just how some things work. And we *are* the closest ER to where I live, so it's bound to happen that I'll see someone I've met at the grocery store or something."

Or something.

Not quite a lie, but close enough.

Thankfully, they'd made it to the swinging doors at that point, and she didn't have to say anything else. As soon as they entered the room, Liz didn't have to wonder who was waiting for Owen.

Hell, even if she hadn't met Murphy that night, she'd have known Owen's family anywhere.

Four men and two women stood up or quit pacing as soon as Liz and Dr. Wilder stepped into the room. Three of the men looked a lot like Owen, and since one was Murphy, she was going to assume that they were the Gallagher brothers. They each had dark hair, beards of various lengths, and ink peeking out in places. The fourth man had a buzz cut and looked dangerous as hell as he hovered by the one Gallagher with the most ink, and a woman with dark hair and full sleeve tattoos.

The other woman in the group stood next to the largest Gallagher with the longest beard. She too had ink and looked just as dangerous as the men.

Hell, the whole crew looked like an ad for a biker gang or something equally as dark and mysterious. Of course, she was doing the one thing she hated: judging them on appearances alone.

Murphy and Owen had been the only two decent guys in a bar filled with idiots and drunken mistakes tonight. Though they were the ones with the most ink, and Owen even had a hoop in his brow, they'd been nice and polite.

Even with the hunger in their eyes.

"They're over there," Liz said softly.

"I could have guessed that," Dr. Wilder said just as softly, and Liz almost tripped. The man *never* joked around, but she was pretty sure she caught the hint of humor in that dry statement.

Tonight was turning even weirder.

"Owen Gallagher's family?" Dr. Wilder asked.

"That's us," the largest said. "We're his family."

"Liz?" Murphy asked, his voice a little hoarse. "You work here?"

She could feel Dr. Wilder's gaze on her, as well as that of the rest of the Gallaghers, and she felt like crawling under the table to avoid their stares. This was *so* not what she needed right now.

"Hello, Murphy. Small world, I know." She tried to keep her voice light, but she knew there would be questions upon questions.

"I'm Dr. Wilder," the man at her side continued. "You seem to know Liz. We worked on your brother."

"Is he okay?" the woman standing between the two men asked.

"He's in surgery now, but we have no reason to believe he won't be up to a hundred percent soon," Dr. Wilder explained.

"Surgery?" the brother with the most ink asked.

"We believe he has a lacerated spleen from the impact of the vehicle, and the surgeons are working diligently on it now. They will be able to tell you more once they finish. In addition to Mr. Gallagher's spleen, he also has a fractured clavicle but it is only a hairline fracture so that is not as bad as it could have been. He also has a mild concussion and two broken ribs, as well as three bruised ones. His recovery will take a bit, but we have no reason to think he won't be back to his normal self, possibly minus a spleen, in no time."

The family let out a breath.

Dr. Wilder's phone beeped, and he frowned as he read the screen. "I'm going to leave Nurse McKinley with you now to answer any questions you may have. You're in good hands with her." He gave Liz a nod and hurried out, leaving her alone with a group of very large men and seemingly even more dangerous women.

How on earth had she ended up in this situation?

"Liz?" Murphy asked.

"How do you know her?" the biggest one asked.

"We met Liz and her friend Tessa tonight," Murphy explained.

"In the bar?" one of the women asked.

"Yes, Blake, in the bar. But Liz didn't drink. Hell, I didn't even finish my beer, and Owen didn't have one at all. We were all just there," Murphy explained. "Liz, this is my brother Graham and his wife, Blake." He pointed to the biggest Gallagher and the woman at his side and then to the next group. "This is Jake and his wife Maya, and their husband, Border." Murphy gave her a look that dared her to make anything of the triad, and she just raised a brow. She worked in a freaking ER; seeing three people who clearly loved and cared about each other didn't even faze her.

"I'd say nice to meet you, but that's never the case in an ER waiting room," she said, and the family relaxed a fracture more. Apparently, she'd passed some kind of test because Graham's eyes held a little bit of respect. She had a feeling this was the eldest brother, and his opinion held sway. Where, she wondered, did Owen fall in the lineup?

"Why don't you guys take a seat?" she asked. "I'm here to answer as many questions as I can before I get called back."

They reluctantly took their seats, and Liz sat next to Blake. Both women studied her, but Liz didn't feel like they were judging in the way some women did. It was more that they were curious but protective. She actually admired that, and was a little jealous that Owen had so many people who cared about him.

Liz had Tessa.

But damn it, that was all she needed.

"I need to check on the baby," Border said. He nodded at Graham and Blake. "I'll make sure Rowan is good, too, though I'm sure they're all still sleeping with Harry and Marie watching over them. I'll be right back."

The family asked Liz a few questions, and she did her best to answer them fully. With Owen still in surgery, she didn't have all the answers, but she could at least talk about recovery time with regards to his other injuries. When her phone buzzed her back, she stood up and took her leave, but not before two detectives came over to talk with the family.

Now she was really curious as to what had happened after she'd left the bar with Tessa, but it wasn't her business. She'd make sure Owen was okay after he got out of surgery because she always checked in on her patients, and then she'd push him from her mind.

After all, he was just a man in a bar. Just a patient.

Nothing more. Nothing less.

And unless she went upstairs to the surgical floor to physically check on him, she'd never see him again.

Good.

Because nothing good could come from seeing Owen Gallagher again.

Nothing.

Chapter Three

Owen knew strangling his sisters-in-law would only make matters worse, but that didn't mean the thought hadn't floated through his mind. Repeatedly. They might be trying to help, but there was only so much a man could take before he started to lose it. It had been over two weeks since that damn car had hit him, and his family was only *now* letting him come home. He'd never missed his bed as much as he did right then.

His incision didn't ache quite as much as it had before, but he still felt like the rest of his internal organs would shift if he moved too fast. Completely insane, he knew, but that didn't stop his imagination from running wild. He still had his arm in a sling so he wouldn't jostle his shoulder, but since the hairline fracture on his collarbone had been minimal, he hadn't needed a cast or something totally binding. In fact, the doctor had said he'd be fine in a couple of weeks as long as he did his physical therapy and didn't lift drywall—something that had actually been on his list of things to do prior to the accident. His doctor had given him the same advice for his ribs regarding movement with time being the key factor in healing. Since he'd been incapacitated thanks to the surgery, his ribs were well on their way to mending themselves.

It had only taken two weeks of constant hovering by his family, and being poked and prodded until his brain felt like it was going to pound right out of his head to get him to this point.

And if his overly loving family didn't leave him the hell alone, he might actually start strangling people with his good hand. It might set back his recovery a few weeks, but it would be worth it.

"Let me get that pillow out of the car," Blake said as she tapped her fingers on her hip, studying him. "I don't think you have enough pillows. I mean you have some decorative ones on the bed, but not enough good ones to keep you steady here on the couch."

"I'm surprised the darn things aren't numbered," Maya mumbled. He was slightly surprised to hear the word darn and not damn coming from Maya's mouth, but as she held her son, Noah, in her arms, he couldn't really blame her. The whole family was trying to keep from cursing so much in front of Noah and Blake's daughter, Rowan, but so far, they hadn't really achieved it. Not surprising since before Jake and Graham had married their significant others, they'd all just been a bunch of bachelors who worked on construction sites or in studios like Jake. Cursing was a way of life.

"I don't number my pillows," Owen growled. "I like things to be organized and labeled, but I don't actually use my label maker for throw pillows."

"So you say," Maya said with a snort. "I might have just missed the tiny numbers hand-sewn into the fabric."

Owen barely held himself back from flipping her off. Lovingly, of course.

Rowan, Blake and Graham's ten-year-old, ran up to them at that moment and held out her arms, a wide smile on her face. "Can I hold Noah? I promise to be careful."

Maya's face softened even as Blake turned to help the exchange. Rowan sat down on the floor next to Owen's overlarge armchair, and Maya handed Noah over. The boy was just big enough to sit up on his own, and he absolutely adored his cousin, Rowan. And though Owen didn't have kids, as soon as Jake had announced that the triad was having a baby, Owen had made sure his home was safe enough for a toddler to run around. Rowan had come along right before then when Graham had married Blake, and now each of the Gallagher homes had toys and games for the kids to play with.

Somehow, the Gallaghers were becoming domesticated, and Owen was just fine with that. It was about time, after all. If his parents had still been alive, they would have joined in on the fun.

His chest ached, and he knew it wasn't from the impact of the car, but from old wounds he knew would never heal. Some things just didn't settle no matter how much time passed, and for that he was grateful. Because without the pain, he was afraid he'd lose the memory of his parents. They'd been everything to him, even though they had spent most of their time with his younger brother since Murphy had been sick more often than not.

And now they weren't around to watch his other brothers find their happiness, and that ate at Owen day by day. He let out a sigh and winced as a dull pain radiated up his side. Hell, broken ribs hurt more than broken bones and surgical incisions. How that was possible, he didn't know, but he was damn tired of it.

"What's wrong?" Murphy asked as he came into the house carrying a walker.

A damned walker. It wasn't as if anyone had let him use it, however. Since he had one arm in a sling and broken ribs down that side, as well, he'd been forced in a wheelchair when he wasn't slowly walking on his own two feet. But some orderly had put a walker on the list of things he might need for recovery, so his brothers had gotten it for him. While Owen appreciated lists—hell, loved them like they were his children—he wasn't a fan of his recovery list.

In fact, that list could go straight to hell along with the driver of the truck that had hit him.

"I'm fine," Owen bit out, angry all over again about what had happened in the parking lot.

"You winced," Murphy accused.

"I was just thinking about the damn truck that hit me." Not quite a lie now, but he wasn't about to let the rest of them act like mother hens. Thankfully, Border, Jake, and Graham were at work, and the others would soon be heading off in that direction also. They'd built a nursery at the tattoo shop where Maya worked so Noah would be going with her, and Rowan was off school thanks to a parent-teacher day and would be accompanying Blake to the shop, as well. Maya co-owned Montgomery Ink, while Blake was the piercer at the shop, though she did some ink on the side. How his brothers had been lucky enough to get the women, Owen didn't know. But right now, he just wanted them out of his damn house.

"Are you okay?" Rowan asked from the floor, Noah in her arms.

Owen had forgotten she was down there when he'd spoken, and now he felt like an ass. While they hadn't hidden what had happened from her since she was too old to keep in the dark, they'd done their best to not scare her.

Good going, Uncle Owen.

"I'm okay," he said with a small smile he hoped reached his eyes. "I promise. I'll be good as new in no time."

Rowan nodded. "Good. But if you need a Band-Aid, let me know. Daddy got me extra pink ones with sparkles because he said you might need some."

Murphy snorted as Owen did his best to not grit his teeth. While his family was worried about the fact that someone had hit him and driven off, and that there were no leads, they also loved giving him shit. Of course, had it been the other way around, he'd be right with them, doing his best to give everyone shit, as well.

He was a Gallagher, after all.

"Okay, I think you have everything you need," Blake said after a moment. "I really wish you'd stay with us a bit longer."

Owen shook his head. He'd been staying at Graham and Blake's because they had a spare bedroom, and Rowan was old enough to deal with him around. He could have stayed at any of his brothers' places, but they all knew he needed to stay at Graham's. His eldest brother needed to make sure all his ducklings were okay, even if Graham would never admit it.

"I'm fine," Owen bit out. "I need to be in my own house, Blake. But I hope you know I'll always be grateful for how much you all helped me. Okay?"

Blake narrowed her eyes. "You're placating me, but I'll take it. Just know that we'll all be stopping by daily because we're mother hens, and you just need to deal with it."

"And you guys thought I was the honest and blunt one," Maya put in.

"There are two of you now," Murphy said with a grin. "God help us all."

Maya punched Murphy's left arm, while Blake punched his right. From the look on Murphy's face, neither woman had held back. Good.

"Dude, I bruise like a peach, be careful with my delicate self," Murphy complained with a shit-eating grin.

"Get out," Owen growled. "I love you, but get out. I

have my computer and can finally get some work done, but I just want to breathe."

Murphy shook his head and reached for Owen's computer. Owen clutched it to his chest and tried not to bash his ribs. "You aren't working, Owen."

"Touch my computer and face my wrath. This is my precious. You don't touch my precious."

The girls snickered and shook their heads. "Owen, you can't work right now," Blake insisted.

"You need to heal," Maya added. "The company isn't going to fall apart without you."

Well, that just wasn't true. He was the manager of the entire company, the one who organized everything. The only reason things were working at all was because Owen had laid everything out for them in color-coded lists and spreadsheets. He'd been working ahead as always, but soon, his brothers would catch up to where he'd left off and go off on their own.

Without him.

Chaos would ensue for sure.

"You don't exactly know that, and I can't just sit on my couch and do *nothing*. I need to work."

Murphy narrowed his eyes. "You can take time off. Graham and I can handle it. And Jake can even help, too."

Owen shook his head and looked down at the kids

before whispering. "It's been over a damn week of me doing *nothing*. I took time off. I'm not an invalid. And we have a deadline coming up on that project both you and Graham have been too busy for. I'm not letting that fall to the wayside because of a little accident."

Fire hit Murphy's eyes, and Owen sighed. "Little? You're calling that a little accident."

Blake let out a breath and bent down to pick up Noah from Rowan's arms. "Let's go make sure Owen's bed is made, honey."

Rowan gave her mother a look that told her she wasn't fooled but followed Blake and Noah to the back of the house where little ears could be spared.

"You can take time off, damn it," Maya put in. "I don't understand why you can't just let other people handle the reins."

"Seriously? You've known me for how long, and you have trouble figuring out that I need to do things? I have lists to create. Calls to make. And emails to ensure haven't been deleted off the company server because Graham and Murphy hate dealing with people."

"Hey."

Owen raised a brow at his brother. "I know you. Don't try deny anything I just said." Owen took a deep breath. "Now let me work in peace. In fact, I'm going to walk you guys out because I'm allowed to get up and move every hour, and this is my time." He held up a hand, happy that his side didn't hurt as he did. "Let me do this. You need to stop treating me like a baby."

"Then stop acting like one," Maya snapped but leaned down to pick up the diaper bag. "Fine. We'll leave you, and we'll even walk you out, but we're still coming back to check on you. It's what we do, and you can't stop us."

"I can try," he mumbled and shut his mouth at Maya's glare. He wiggled himself off the couch, aware that the others were watching him for every deep intake of breath, every wince. He'd let the pain get to him later because, first, he needed to get the others out of the house so he could function.

Yes, he'd been hit by a car, but it could have been way worse.

He would be fine.

Fine.

Finally on two feet, he gestured with his good arm for the others to lead the way out. Maya held Noah, as Blake made sure Rowan had all her things. Murphy kept an eye on Owen since his little brother refused to let Owen walk alone. Sure, Owen probably would have done the same thing if Murphy were in his position, but still.

When they'd made it to the porch, Owen looked

over, surprised to see a moving truck in his neighbor's driveway.

"Looks like your new neighbor is finally settling in," Blake said. "I would have thought they'd have gotten their stuff before now."

Owen almost shrugged but thought better of it at the last moment. "I was busy before the accident, and I think whoever moved next door must have been too because I haven't even seen them yet. They may have been around more this last week, but I wasn't here. Maybe it just took them this long to find time for the movers or something." He could understand that since his job tended to take over his life, as well. Not that it had recently since the others had cut him off. However, that would change just as soon as his family got in their vehicles and left.

He looked over at the other house again and froze when a familiar blonde head popped up from behind the truck. His heart raced and his throat went dry. Holy hell.

"Holy shit," Murphy murmured from his side. "Is that the hot nurse from the bar? Liz, right?"

Maya leaned over so she and Noah could get a better look and smiled. "Well, look at that."

"You didn't know she'd moved next door?" Blake asked.

"No," Owen said softly, trying to get his brain to catch up with the rest of him. Hell, he'd forgotten how beautiful she was, considering he hadn't seen her since they wheeled him away for surgery, and he'd been a little drugged up at that point. He wasn't drugged up now and his dick was about to stand at attention just at the mere sight of her. "Maybe she's just helping her friend?"

The brunette from the bar walked out of the house at that point, and Murphy let out a soft laugh. "Maybe Tessa moved next door instead. Come on, man, let's go meet the neighbors." Murphy turned to him. "You okay to walk, or do you need me to grab the wheelchair."

Owen set his jaw. "I'm good." He would be, damn it, even if he ended up sweating through his shirt from the exertion. He wasn't in that much pain, it was just uncomfortable. Thankfully, his incision site barely hurt anymore. And since he'd caught sight of Liz, he wasn't thinking about pain. No, the endorphins running through his system just from seeing her were taking care of any discomfort he might have.

"Hey, ladies," Murphy called out, and Blake sighed from Owen's side.

"He is seriously going to flirt with your neighbors right now on their moving day," Blake said with a laugh. "You can't take him anywhere, can you?"

"That's why we love him," Owen said with a smile. Of course, he only had eyes for Liz at that moment, who had turned at the sound of Murphy's voice to look at them. Her eyes had gone wide, and her face paled slightly. He hoped she was just surprised because going pale at the sight of him wasn't the reaction he had hoped for, and definitely not the best way to start things.

Start things?

What the hell was he talking about? This was his new neighbor, not someone he was going to *start* something with. He needed to get his head on straight.

"Murphy?" Tessa asked as she came to Liz's side. "You live here? Small world."

Murphy shook his head. "No, Owen lives next door. We were just here to drop him off."

Tessa winced. "I'm glad to see you on your feet, Owen. I heard about what happened. I hope you're doing better."

Owen nodded, his eyes on Liz, who still hadn't said anything. Come to think of it, he hadn't said anything either. "Thanks. I'm doing much better. In fact, I get to actually stay home today and let everyone else get back to their lives. I was staying with Graham and Blake so they could hover over me."

Blake snorted. "You need some hovering every once in a while. This is Rowan, my daughter, and the little guy in Maya's arms is her son, Noah. So, who moved next door? Can we help?"

Liz blinked, finally seeming to come out of whatever trance she'd been in when they'd walked over. "Hi. Actually, Tessa and I both moved in. We bought the house together."

Tessa grinned and put her arm around Liz's shoulders. "We've been friends and roommates since college, and since finding a decent house these days is killer, we decided to go in on this one together. It's not quite a fixer-upper, but it's not perfect yet either."

Liz sighed. "We actually have movers to help. But, thank you. The guys are on their lunch break, so Tessa and I were just making sure that what they had left was labeled correctly so it could be put into the right rooms."

Owen grinned then. Nothing made him happier than knowing someone else labeled things like he did. And honestly, who would move without making sure their boxes were perfectly labeled?

"Did you color-code, too?" Murphy asked. "When we moved Owen into his place a few years back, he'd labeled each box with a different color so we knew where to put things. Of course, he hired *us* to move him in and not someone else since he didn't trust anyone except a Gallagher to do things."

Owen rolled his eyes at Murphy's words and Liz's

questioning look. "We own a restoration and construction company. We had the manpower and the truck. Of course, I made my family help. And, really, if you need anything, just let us know. I'm right next door."

Liz raised a brow and looked down at his sling. "Shouldn't you be resting instead of offering to help lift boxes?"

Owen just grinned. His dick was hard, and his ribs hurt because his dick was hard. He couldn't help it if Liz did this to him. Of course, now he had images of Nurse Liz in his mind, playing doctor and patient with him despite knowing it was all kinds of wrong.

"I wouldn't lift boxes, I'd just help you keep organized."

Liz shook her head. "I'm plenty organized for the both of us, thank you." She looked down at her phone and frowned. "And the movers should be back in a moment, so I'll let you guys go about your business. It's a small, small world that you're our neighbor, Owen. But I'm glad you're up and walking around."

And with that, he and his family were dismissed. Owen gave Liz a nod and lifted his chin toward Tessa before he turned back. Murphy gave him a strange look, but he shook his head. He didn't know why Liz didn't seem to like him much, and he couldn't really deal with it right then. He needed to heal, needed to make sure this new job went smoothly, and he needed to get his head on straight after knowing someone had hit him with a freaking truck.

All indications pointed to it being intentional, and he still didn't know why someone would do that. Nor did he have any answers. While he would have liked to think it was an accident, the police weren't so optimistic. The forensics and the fact that Owen had been alone in the parking lot, standing under a street lamp, led the authorities to believe that someone had actually hit him on purpose.

And Owen had no idea why.

"We're heading out," Blake said as she pressed Rowan to her side. "You *will* call us if you need anything. And we *will* be back to check on you." She leaned over to kiss his cheek, and Owen sighed. He felt like an ass because he needed his space, but he truly couldn't stand being hemmed in anymore.

"I'm grateful that you guys helped me, that you were there for me," Owen said after a moment. "Hell, I know I couldn't have done anything on my own those first few days. So, thank you, okay? But I need to be me for a bit."

Blake kissed his cheek once more and backed up, giving Rowan room to give him a gentle hug. "Be safe, Owen. You're one of my favorite Gallaghers."

"Hey!" Murphy called out. "I thought I was your favorite."

Blake shook her head and pulled Rowan toward her car. "You're a favorite to someone, I'm sure."

Murphy pressed his hand over his heart and took a step back. "Ouch." He nodded at Owen before saying, "Be good. I'll be back to check on you soon."

"Don't work too hard!" Maya called out as she walked away with Murphy, a waving Noah in her arms.

Owen lifted his good arm and waved back before heading into the house, purposely not looking over at Liz and Tessa's new home. He still couldn't quite believe that they'd moved next door. He'd been sure he wouldn't ever see the two of them again after leaving the bar, and having Liz as his nurse that night had been weird as hell. Now they lived in the next house over?

Maybe the universe was trying to tell him something.

Or maybe he just needed a nap.

His side aching, he made his way through the house and onto the couch. He hadn't overdone it yet from just walking outside, but he knew if he weren't careful, he'd end up hurting himself more and have to take more time off from the jobsite. That was the last thing he wanted to do, so he would just take the rest of the day to sit on the couch and work from his laptop. Using his brain wasn't going to hurt anything else.

He hoped.

As soon as he settled into the couch with his laptop, tablet, and cell phone ready to go, someone knocked on the door. He closed his eyes and let out a curse, figuring it had to be one of his well-meaning family members. They couldn't let him have ten minutes to himself, apparently. If he didn't love them as much as he did, he might start to hate them.

"It's open!" he called out, not in the mood to deal with getting up again.

There was a slight hesitation before the door slowly opened, and a blonde head peeked around the door.

"Do you just let anyone into your house?" Liz asked, a furrow between her brows.

Owen swallowed hard and tried to move things around to stand up. "Uh, sorry. I thought you were a Gallagher checking in on me."

Liz shook her head and held out a hand as she moved fully into his living room. "Didn't they just leave? Don't get up. Please. I promise I won't be long." She strolled inside in that no-nonsense way of hers with a container of cookies in one hand.

He studied the way she moved, the way she stared at him as if she couldn't quite make out exactly who or even *what* he was, and he found himself liking it. He was either really hard up for someone, or this woman truly intrigued him. He would go with the latter.

Owen shook himself out of his thoughts and set his laptop down on the coffee table, doing his best to avoid twisting too much. He wasn't sure he'd be able to hold back the wince if he moved more than necessary.

"Hi," he said after a moment, an awkward feeling setting in.

"Hi," she said with a sigh and set down the container of cookies. "We had an extra box from when Tessa and I went a little crazy on junk food, and I—we—figured that you could use the sugar since you've been down for the count for a bit. I know cookies aren't the best fuel for healing, but sometimes a little sugar goes a long way. And I know that they aren't homemade or anything, but Tessa and I work long hours, and we're lucky to even have these in the pantry."

He looked down at the box and then back up at her. "I thought I was the one who was supposed to bring over cookies to the new neighbors."

She shrugged. "Well, they're feel-better cookies. As well as I'm-sorry-I-was-acting-like-a-bitch-to-you cookies." She held up her chin at that point, and he snorted before wincing. Okay, so snorting wasn't on his approved list of things to do when in pain.

"You're not a bitch."

"Didn't say I was. I said I was sorry for *acting* like one." She smiled as she said it, and he shook his head, annoyed with himself for liking her so much.

"You shouldn't be sorry, then," Owen put in. "Every time I've seen you, which seems to be a lot considering we don't know each other, you've been in the middle of something when I barge in—this last time with most of my family members. So I can't really blame you for not wanting me around. I'm encroaching." And he wanted to encroach more.

She shuffled from foot to foot, and he had a feeling she'd planned out her speech and didn't know what to do after that. He still didn't quite understand why she was here, but he found he liked it.

They'd had three very different encounters until now, and for some reason, he had a feeling that meant something. Of course, from the way she kept looking around, he also felt that she wanted to walk right out the door and never look back.

"Well, I hope you feel better. I left Tessa alone with the movers, so I need to make sure they're in one piece. Bye, Owen. Heal well."

"Thanks for the cookies, Liz."

She gave him a quick nod before turning and walking out of his house, flipping the lock as she did. He had a feeling she didn't truly want to look back and see him again. After all, he was just some guy from a bar, just some guy who'd gotten hit by a car, and now, just some guy who lived next door.

He wasn't anything to her.

And yet, for some reason, she intrigued him enough that he wanted her to be something to him.

The pain in his ribs pulsed, and he cursed. Before he did anything, however, he needed to heal. Needed to be the Owen he used to be, where he could handle anything without passing out from just walking to the bathroom.

He'd get there, damn it, because if he didn't, he might just go crazy.

Chapter Four

Liz's back ached and her feet were going numb, but she figured that was just all in a day's work. Thankfully, she was only working an eight-hour shift today since she was about to hit heavy overtime, and her boss would start yelling after that. And there was another nurse on call so they wouldn't be shorthanded, but if the ER got too busy, Liz had a feeling she'd be called right back in, labor laws or no.

How the hell the place would run with one less nurse due to budget cutbacks, she didn't know. They barely handled things as it was.

The sound of heels clicking on tile brought Liz out of her increasingly depressing thoughts, and she turned to watch Tessa make her way to the desk area. She held a stack of folders against her chest and had two to-go cups of coffee in her hands.

"You're not usually down here this time of day," Liz said as Tessa set down a cup in front of Liz. She greedily took the cup and sipped the sweet brew. The admin offices always had better coffee than the nurses' station. Hell, they had better *everything*.

Even Tessa's outfit was better than Liz's scrubs could ever hope to be. Her friend wore a dark coal pencil skirt and a matching, tailored jacket with a maroon top. Even her shoes were cute and pointy and had a heel that Liz was pretty sure she'd break an ankle in. Liz's orthopedics weren't fancy, but they kept her feet from throbbing an hour in. Since she was on hour seven, she couldn't really blame her arches for screaming right about then. It had been a long day, and she still had a bunch of paperwork to finish before she called it a night.

"I had a few things to talk over, so I figured I'd bring some coffee when I came," Tessa explained. Her friend worked in the insurance department of the administrative offices. The dichotomy of her party-girl friend turning into the shark businesswoman who fought for the rights of her patients always made Liz smile. "Did you see Dr. Wilder today?" Tessa asked with a grin.

"He's looking all manly and on the good side of haggard."

Liz almost snorted her drink and shook her head as she looked around to make sure no one was listening in. Thankfully, it was just the two of them since everyone was in their rooms actually doing work. Liz had a few moments to breathe before she had to move, but she was still making sure everything was logged into the computer correctly.

"What is the 'good side of haggard?'" Liz asked, knowing she probably shouldn't egg on Tessa. Nothing good ever came from that, other than a laugh or two. In the end, Liz usually ended up beet-red and trying to hide from embarrassment. According to Tessa, Liz needed more of that in her life. But that's why they were friends.

Tessa rolled her eyes and gestured with her coffee. "You know, the five o'clock shadow and the way a man has to stretch because his lower back is hurting? It's all you can do to keep from reaching out to help." She wiggled her brows, and Liz let out a groan.

"You're terrible, you know that?"

"True, but I'm not the only one thinking it. Lisa, of course, was saying it earlier in the break room, and with many dirty words involved."

Liz held back her snarl as she took another sip. "I don't even want to know."

"Suit yourself. But you should probably know that she was also telling anyone who would listen that you're having a secret love affair with a patient." Fire came into Tessa's eyes, and Liz wanted to bang her head against the computer screen.

"Are you serious?" Liz whispered. "It's been how long since Owen came in, and he's not even my patient anymore."

"No, he's just your neighbor. And, by the way, I didn't say it was Owen. You're the one who went there." She smiled softly. "Is there something I should know? You were at his house awhile yesterday with those...cookies."

Liz huffed out a breath and looked around again for anyone who loved gossip. Thankfully, they still had a few minutes. "Shut it. I was there for all of four minutes, and *nothing* happened. Nothing will. I don't date guys like him."

"First of all, you don't date ever. And what do you mean 'guys like him?' Guys who have jobs, are sexy as hell, and clearly available from the way he kept looking at you?"

Liz pinched the bridge of her nose. "It hasn't been *that* long since I went out on a date." A lie. "And just because he looked at me like that doesn't mean he's single." She paused. "Not that he looked at me in any way that implied interest. Because he wasn't. Isn't."

Tessa laughed. "Way to confuse yourself right then, baby girl. Whatever you need to tell yourself..." Her phone beeped, and she crossed her eyes. "Okay, break is over. I need to go meet with a patient. Wish me luck."

"Good luck," Liz said under her breath, and Tessa sauntered off. She truly did not envy Tessa her job. But if anyone could make dealing with astronomical medical bills sympathetic, Tessa could do it. The other woman always did everything she could to make sure people weren't taken advantage of. That couldn't be said for some of the others in her line of work.

"Was that Tessa?" Lisa asked as she came up to the station, her eyes bright.

Liz nodded and drank down the last of her coffee before throwing the cup in recycling. "Yep."

"I wish she'd thought to bring coffee for all of us," Lisa complained. "It's not fair that you get the good stuff while we have to drink the sludge."

As Lisa usually got the fancy drinks from the barista next door for free because she smiled just right, Liz couldn't really find any pity for the other woman. It was just coffee for freak's sake.

"She only has two hands, and since Tessa's my

roommate, I guess I get some perks." Liz shrugged, not in the mood to deal with the other woman. She used to have a longer fuse, but hell, Lisa had been annoying as hell about Owen ever since he'd come into the emergency room, and she honestly didn't care anymore. As long as she did her job and made sure her patients had everything they needed, she'd be okay.

That's all she could do, after all.

"I guess so," Lisa mumbled. "So, have you seen your mystery patient recently? Owen Gallagher, right?"

Liz pinched the bridge of her nose. "I don't know why I would, Lisa. He was just a patient, and you know we don't talk about their procedures."

"If you say so." With that, Lisa sauntered off toward the break room, and Liz tried to compose herself once more.

There was no way in hell she would mention that Owen lived next door to her...all rumpled and grumpy that he wasn't up to a hundred percent yet. Though, in reality, he was doing far better than she'd expected, considering he'd lost his spleen, had a fractured collarbone, and cracked and bruised ribs from the accident.

She didn't know if they'd caught the guy who hit him yet, or if it had even truly been an accident. It wasn't her business, and she hadn't wanted to call in favors to ask about it. Not only would it be highly unethical, it would also draw attention to her that she didn't want. She needed to keep this damn job since it was the only thing she had beyond Tessa.

And wasn't that a sad thought.

Liz rolled her shoulders and looked at the board before picking up her things. A new patient had been put in one of her rooms when she'd been talking to Lisa, and since the orderly was now out of the way, she'd go in and see what needed to be done.

What she hadn't expected was to recognize the man on the bed, a pained expression on his face.

"Murphy?" she said with a blink.

He winced and held up a bandaged hand. "Hey, Liz. Fancy meeting you here."

She shook her head and made her way to his side. "What on earth did you do?"

"Got a little too close to a wall that decided it needed to come down right then. A piece of metal got me, and Graham sent me over here with one of the guys. I think I got the bleeding stopped, but since it took a while, I figured I might need stitches."

She shook her head as she looked at the wound on his hand. "I'm glad the bleeding stopped for now, but I think the doctor will want to stitch you up for sure." She wrapped his hand again and started his vitals. "You Gallaghers sure like coming into my ER."

Murphy grinned, making him look far younger than his brothers. Of course, if she remembered right, he *was* the youngest. She just didn't know his exact age. "We just like you, I guess. How's the new house coming along?"

She shrugged as she worked, noting his pulse rate and BP. "Slowly. Okay, I'm going, to get the doctor in here ASAP because I want to see what he has to say Is there anyone in the waiting room for you?" Had Owen somehow gotten himself there, sling and all? Not that she said that last part.

Murphy shook his head. "The guy had to drop me off since we're behind at the job. Jake is on his way, though since he was at home working on a project."

"He doesn't work with you guys?" Why was she so chatty all of a sudden? Maybe she was too tired from her shift and losing it.

"Sometimes he does, but he's actually an artist by trade. He built a whole studio in his house, though I think they're building on even more now that they have Noah and three adults living in the place. Anyway, Graham called him and Owen to make sure the family knew I'd been an idiot with a falling wall, and since Owen can't drive yet, Jake's on his way."

"It's nice that you have so many people who care

about you." Liz at least had Tessa, but that was all she needed.

And maybe if she kept telling herself that, she might start to believe it fully one day.

"They're all a little overprotective, but I can't really blame them considering how I grew up." He shrugged, but the look on his face right then didn't make her want to ask him what exactly he was talking about.

She knew far too much about the Gallaghers as it was, and she needed to be careful. Not only to protect herself but also to protect her job. She couldn't be too friendly with her patients, not when Lisa and Nancy were watching her like gossipy hawks.

"Well, I'll get the doctor in here right away. How is your pain level right now?"

"I've had worse," Murphy answered, and she had a feeling he wasn't trying to be tough just then.

"How about you give me a number between one and ten about your pain. Just in case."

"Like a four, I guess. It hurt when it happened, but now it's just a dull throb."

She nodded and noted that down. "I'll be right back, okay? And if it's not me, Jennifer is coming on shift soon and is taking over my patients. You'll be in good hands."

Murphy smiled then. "I'm not sure Owen would want me to be in your hands. Just saying."

Someone cleared his or her throat at the edge of the curtain, and Liz mentally cursed herself for standing there too long.

"Yes, Lisa?" Liz asked as she turned to the other woman.

Lisa smiled brightly. "Oh, nothing, I was just letting you know that Jennifer is here. Go about your business." She waved them off before practically skipping to the nurses' station. Dear God, it was like high school all over again, and Liz had no way out.

"Did I get you in trouble?" Murphy asked, genuine concern in his voice.

"No, I think I did that all on my own," she blurted without thinking. She let out a breath and went over his chart one more time. "Never mind. Okay, let me get the doctor for you, and Jennifer will be in, as well. You're going to be fine, Murphy."

"I know," he agreed. "You're good at what you do. Just ask Owen."

She shook herself. "That is something I won't be doing, but thank you." And with that, she walked out of his room and did her job, ignoring the way Lisa watched her.

She couldn't let the other woman get to her, not when she had to work her ass off since they were both competing for the same thing—to stay in their positions when the budget went off the rails.

She just prayed she didn't make any more mistakes. She couldn't afford it.

No matter how many Gallaghers life seemed to want to throw at her.

* * *

Owen was a new man. Or, at least, mostly a new man. It had been another week, and now he was able to move around without wanting to cry, his incision didn't hurt at all, and his arm might still be in a sling, but his collar and shoulder didn't ache. His brothers might not let him drive yet thanks to the sling, but he was well and truly on his way to being healed.

Thank. God.

The sounds of men and women cursing and hitting things with hammers filled his ears, and he wanted to close his eyes and sway to that version of music. The smell of concrete being poured and finished wood hit him hard, and he wanted to go down on his knees and weep.

It had been far too long since he'd been allowed on any of their jobsites, and all he wanted to do was stay there forever and remember why he loved working at Gallagher Brothers Restoration.

"You look ready to either cry or start humping the drywall," Graham said as he made his way to Owen's side. "I don't know if either one is really workplace appropriate."

Owen flipped his brother off with his good arm and smiled. "I won't cry yet, and I'm not that into drywall. That sounds more of a you thing, to be honest."

Graham went to punch Owen's shoulder and thought better of it. "As soon as you're healed, I'll hit you."

"Thank you," he said dryly. "I'd hate to think you'd have to hold yourself back for years."

Graham snorted. "Like any of us could hold back for that long. You're lucky you have that sling on today to remind us since any road rash you still have is covered by that button-down shirt you have on. Could you look more out of place right now, dude?"

"Shut up. It was easier to put this on than something over my head," Owen explained. "Plus, you guys won't let me work with anything out there, so I'll be in the trailer most of the day anyway, working on whatever mess you guys left for me."

"First, it's called insurance, dumbass. I'm not about

to let you get hurt even worse on the jobsite because you're an idiot. Second, we didn't mess things up."

Owen raised a brow. "I saw what Murphy did to my spreadsheet. He's lucky he's far away right now, or I'd kick his ass. I'm honestly a little scared to look at what you guys did to my desk."

Graham gave Owen a guilty look and suddenly had a fascination with his boots. "You might want to fortify yourself."

Owen groaned. "What did you do?"

"Nothing," Graham said quickly. Too quickly. "You know how much Murphy hates sticky notes."

Owen closed his eyes and counted to five. "You aren't that big of a fan yourself. I'm forever finding little pieces of paper scattered around that I need to organize."

Graham winced. "Well...at least you're used to things like that. Maybe it will help calm you after a while. You know, like organizing for the soul or some crap like that. It'll keep you at the desk and not near a hammer, at least."

This time, Owen counted to ten.

"You should go back to whatever He-Man thing you were doing before Jake dropped me off because I don't think you want to be near me once I go in there. Right?"

Graham backed away slowly with his hands raised—

funny since the man had a couple of inches on him and twenty pounds of muscle. "You got it. I'll send Jake in later to get you for lunch. How's that?"

Graham didn't even wait for Owen to answer before he was off and out of the way of Owen's fist. Not that Owen could really hit the man right then since he wasn't up to hundred percent yet, but hell, if Graham could delay hitting Owen, then Owen could wait to hit Graham. Owen would be sure to keep a list of infractions so he could get his big brother back.

He made his way to the trailer and up the old, wooden steps, doing his best to not think about what he was about to see. It couldn't be that, bad, right? He'd only been gone a couple of weeks.

He opened the door and froze.

Yeah, it could be that bad.

And worse.

All of Owen's notebooks were splayed out on two desks, his keyboard lying unevenly on top of a few that were stacked. Countless pieces of paper with notes jotted in ink, pencil, and what looked like crayon covered the tables and desks.

The large pile of sticky notes seemed to be untouched.

Owen once again counted to ten before closing the

door behind him and readying himself. Well, at least he wouldn't be bored on his first day back.

No, he would just be angry.

And would get organized.

By the time lunch rolled around, he at least had everything in organized stacks. He was just finishing entering a few things into the computer when Jake strolled in, his hair a mess and dark circles under his eyes. He'd looked pretty much the same when he'd come to pick up Owen that morning.

"Need more coffee?" he asked his older brother, concern in his voice.

"That's all I'm running on," Jake said with a yawn. "Sorry. I had a huge project run over, and Noah has a slight cold. And because Maya needed her sleep since Austin is on vacation from the shop this week, Border and I stayed up with Noah. But, of course, Maya couldn't just sleep, she had to come in and out of the nursery all night, freaking out, so Border and I had to make sure Maya was taken care of, as well. It all added up to a very long night, and not enough sleep for anyone."

Owen pointed to the chair next to him with his good

arm. "Sit, man. Why are you here if you're so tired? You're allowed to sleep, you know."

Jake sank into the chair and tilted his head back so he could rest. "With Murphy down a hand thanks to those stitches, and you out, as well, Graham needed someone. I know I usually only do the intricate things at the end, but Dad trained all of us, so I know how to help with the actual construction. I don't want to let you guys down."

"You never have, Jake. And you won't."

Considering Owen was the one who worked the least with his hands these days—even before the accident—he was pretty sure *he* was the one that let people down. But as soon as this next project came through, he'd make sure that was a thing of the past. He might not be as handy as the rest of his brothers most days, but he could at least do this.

And as soon as he had his client meeting later that day, he knew he'd be back on track. No truck with bright headlights and the subsequent unending pain would change that.

Jake let out a deep breath before pulling himself out of the chair. "Okay, Graham sent me in to force you outside so you can eat with the rest of them. So let's get to it because Graham gets grumpy without food."

Owen snorted as he stood up, pocketing his phone

and making sure he had his tablet in his messenger bag as he did. "Graham gets grumpy regardless, full stomach or not."

Jake grinned over his shoulder. "True, though Blake and Rowan are helping that."

Owen followed his brother out, wondering why those words made him a little jealous. Graham had his new family that kept him sane, while Jake had everything he ever wanted—even though Owen was pretty sure Jake had never thought a triad would be his future.

Now Owen and Murphy were the only single ones left, and while he used to think that was just fine since he hadn't been ready to settle down, Owen was feeling just a bit too lonely for his tastes. Maybe it was just because he'd been stuck on the couch for too long and not able to be in his element. Once he was fully immersed back in the land of the living and planners, he'd be back to where he needed to be.

Jake led him down the street less than a block away to the taco joint the crew had fallen in love with when they started this project. Deep and abiding love. It used to be that everyone just brought their lunch and called it a day, but this place had reasonable prices for fucking amazing food. He was pretty sure a quarter of the place's business the past couple of months had come from the Gallaghers and their crew, and Owen couldn't really blame anyone for that.

Once he had his four steak tacos and a soda on his tray, he made his way back to the table. Normally, he wouldn't even need a tray, but if his brothers caught him trying to move around without his sling, he'd get his ass kicked. Graham and Jake were already seated, scarfing down their tacos and not bothering to talk. Who needed conversation when they had this kind of food?

Owen had one *carne asada* down and the other in his hand when Murphy finally made his way to the table, a scowl on his face and his bandaged hand pressed to his chest.

"You okay?" Jake asked around a mouthful of pork taco with extra onions.

"My fucking hand hurts," Murphy growled low before using his left hand to start eating. Considering that all of them were right-handed, Murphy had to be getting annoyed at this point.

"It hasn't been that long since you got your stitches," Graham said slowly. "You're not healed yet."

"I know that," Murphy bit out. "They're just starting to itch, and it's killing me that I can't do anything about it. Liz said I should be fine, and the doctor agreed, but I want to get this damn bandage off so I can go about my business."

Owen choked on his soda and coughed as he tried to catch his breath. "Liz?"

Murphy's eyes brightened as he set down his drink. "Oh, right, I haven't talked to you really since it happened. Yeah, Liz was my nurse." He grinned. "Too bad she was going off shift before I could ask her if she wanted to play nurse with me."

Owen let out a growl before he caught himself. "Don't talk about her like that."

Jake and Graham shared a look but stayed out of it.

"Why, big brother, got a crush?"

"Murphy," Owen warned. "Watch it."

Murphy just grinned. "Oh, get over yourself. I didn't do anything to her and didn't say anything that would make her feel uncomfortable. She was working for freak's sake. All I'm saying, brother mine, is that maybe you should do something about that jealous streak of yours when it comes to your new sexy neighbor instead of growling at me for letting her look at my hand when I was in the ER."

Once again, Jake and Graham shared a look, and Owen wanted to throw something at them. He didn't know why he had this fascination with Liz, but he knew that one day soon, he would either have to forget about it completely or actually do something about it.

"If you're done ragging on me, I'm going to finish

eating so I can get back to work. And don't think I've forgotten the mess you guys left for me."

"You like organizing things," Graham explained. "Think of it as a welcome back present."

Owen flipped him off and continued to eat, ignoring the way his brothers continued to tease him. Well, at least things were getting back to normal. His brothers were being assholes, and he was making lists on what to do about them and the job.

Getting hit by a car could only slow him down so much, damn it. Soon, he'd be back to fighting form and then...and then he might just see how friendly his neighbor would let him be.

Chapter Five

Water slid over her skin, and she moaned, wishing her hand were something far better than it was just then. Liz needed to come, and for some reason, she couldn't get there that morning.

It probably had something to do with the fact that every time a certain bearded and inked neighbor slid into her mind, she pushed him right back out, interrupting any thoughts of orgasm along the way. She'd already washed her hair and the rest of her body, as well as shaved her legs—something she hated when only half awake—and had decided to at least try and get herself off a little bit before the rest of the day. She had a rare day off and wanted to unpack some more and maybe even do something others called relaxing.

But before she could relax, she wanted to have just a tiny bit of bliss.

If only she could get Owen out of her mind.

And at that thought, images of him on his knees in the shower in front of her slid into her mind, and she was powerless to stop them. He had his big, calloused hands on her thighs, slowly squeezing into her flesh before spreading her before him. He'd lick up her inner thigh and the place where her leg met her hip before nibbling down to her mound. His beard would scrape her skin in that sensual way that sent shivers down her spine, and he'd lick her as he kept his eyes up, wanting to see her face as he tasted her.

She'd run her hand through his hair and press him closer, loving the way he sucked on her clit before biting down. She'd throw her head back into the tile, holding onto the soap dish with one hand as she came so she wouldn't fall.

And as she rubbed her hand furiously against her clit, she came, thinking of Owen's mouth on her pussy, his hands molded to her flesh. Her legs shook, and she forced herself to slide down and sit on the floor so she didn't fall and break something.

That was one thing she did *not* want to explain to her coworkers at the ER.

With a fumbling grace, she reached up for the nozzle and turned off the cooling shower, her chest heaving as she tried to catch her breath.

Holy hell.

She'd come freaking *hard* just thinking of Owen Gallagher—a man she should *not* be thinking about at all. He was only her neighbor and a former patient. Nothing more. She didn't even know the man, and for some reason, every time she was around him, he put her back up. She had no idea why, but if some internal part of her wanted to push him away, she should just go with that and ignore any attraction that flared between them.

And that meant no more getting herself off to thoughts of his mouth on her pussy.

Her clit throbbed, and she glared down between her legs.

"For the love of Pete. You just got off. Stop wanting more."

And she'd officially gone crazy. She'd just chastised her clit for daring to want a Gallagher to get her off. And not just any Gallagher. Owen freaking Gallagher. With that sad thought, she pulled herself up and got out of the shower, standing on the rug and toweling off so she wouldn't end up with a puddle in the middle of the floor and slip on it later. She'd seen so many household accidents run through her ER that she tried her best to not become a statistic. With a sigh, she pushed those unhealthy thoughts from her mind and went about making a mental list for the day. There were still countless things to do around the house to get it fully unpacked and looking like a home. Standing around naked in her bathroom was not one of them.

By the time she got dressed and headed into the kitchen to make coffee, her list had grown past a mental one, and she was already writing things down in order on her phone. She didn't know what she would do without the note app and the ability to move things around on it. As she sipped her coffee, she looked around her new kitchen and let herself smile. They might not be completely unpacked, and she and Tessa would have to move things around to paint in a year or so, but it was *hers*.

She no longer had to pay rent, and she didn't have to deal with landlords who liked looking at her breasts rather than her face, or never being able to change anything because she didn't own it. And while it was Tessa's first home, as well, Liz had *never* truly owned anything in her life at all. This place and all its faults were hers, and she couldn't wait to put her stamp on it.

Tessa had left early that morning for work so today

would be Liz's day to put things to rights. They had a master list they worked from so they didn't redo things or miss something important—thankfully, Tessa loved lists as much as she did. Tessa might be a little wilder than Liz, but she loved order in some things just as much as Liz.

Liz carried her coffee toward the front of the house, wanting to do something she quite possibly had never done in her life—sit on her front porch and take in the morning. That had always seemed so...unproductive to her, and while it still probably was, she was going to try it out if only for one morning.

Tessa had brought home the ugliest outdoor chairs Liz had ever set eyes on to put on their front porch. They didn't match each other, let alone the house, or the set they had in the back yard. Liz wanted to either upholster and paint them or get rid of them altogether, but Tessa would hear nothing of the sort. Apparently, it was Tessa's project, and Liz would just have to deal with it.

This is what came with buying a house with your friend and not your spouse.

Liz shrugged as she sank into the surprisingly comfortable chair. She'd just get her way on something else inside the house since that's how they worked. She sighed and took another sip of her coffee. Even though they were ugly, the chairs weren't uncomfortable. In fact, the one she rested in seemed to mold to her butt quite perfectly, and now she didn't want to get up.

Maybe Tessa had a plan, after all.

The morning was just settling in, and from her position on the porch, she could see the beauty of the Rocky Mountains as well as the foothills that seemed so much closer in their new place than in the small apartment they used to share. She'd wanted this house because of the view alone, and Tessa had been right there with her. There was truly nothing as majestic and beautiful than the Rockies on a clear morning.

As soon as that thought had entered her mind, a certain bearded neighbor filled her vision. But this time, it wasn't just her imagination. He'd taken off his sling and wore a tight t-shirt as well as a worn pair of jeans that clung to his very thick and muscled thighs as well as that firm butt of his that made her mouth water. She wasn't sure if he could see her from where he stood, but the fact that he probably couldn't made her feel like a lecher.

That didn't stop her from staring, however.

She took another sip of her coffee, her gaze no longer on the mountains but on the man she'd just come thinking about. The man she *shouldn't* be thinking about at all. He was too close to her life, too gruff, too... just too everything. When she was ready to settle down, she'd find a nice, calm man that didn't make her go crazy for no reason. She didn't want to be with a man with large hands that could use them for any purpose he desired.

Liz closed her eyes and let out a breath, pushing those thoughts from her mind. She hadn't thought about those days for a while now, and she wouldn't start now. And for one thing, she above all others knew that it didn't take a man with large hands to inflict the kind of pain she tried not to think about.

Smaller hands with a firm disposition could do well enough if they wanted to.

Especially on someone much smaller.

The coffee now bitter on her tongue, she set her cup down on the small table that separated the two armchairs. It wasn't very stable, but as long as she kept the mug in the center and didn't wobble the table, it should be fine.

Liz rubbed her temples, trying to get her mind into gear and out of the past, but it wasn't easy. She didn't know why she kept thinking about that, especially since it had been so long since she'd dealt with any of it, but, apparently, her brain didn't want to quit down that path anytime soon.

Determined to think of other things, she looked up right at the same moment that Owen did, but instead of making eye contact, he went down like a bag of bricks. His muffled oath reached her ears as she jumped out of her chair and ran toward him.

"Owen?" she called out, her bare feet pounding through the grass, the morning dew sliding over her skin.

"I'm fine," he groaned, rolling over onto his back. "Just tripped over the damn newspaper that I canceled a year ago and they keep periodically sending." He had his eyes closed and his good arm up and over his forehead. His other one, however, lay at his side stiffly. He'd bent one leg up, the other one lying straight while he took in deep breaths.

She went to her knees at his side and shook her head. "You shouldn't be out and about yet. And you *really* shouldn't be without your sling."

Owen cracked open an eye and glared at her. "Actually, I'm allowed to do both in small bursts. I figured going out to check the mail I didn't have a chance to get yesterday because I got home too late would be a good time to do it. But since I was barefoot and stupid, I tripped." He groaned as he lifted his bad arm, but she didn't see any signs of shocking pain over his face.

"Don't move," Liz ordered. "Let me check you over."

Owen smiled then. "You're welcome to check me out, Nurse Liz."

She rolled her eyes, forcing herself not to smile. Damn man always got under her skin, and not always in a bad way. "Let me know if this hurts."

She poked and prodded him, but he didn't move out of her way. If anything, he leaned into her touch, and she forced herself not to keep her hands on him for long. Damn it, she needed to keep this professional. It didn't matter that they weren't in the hospital. She had a responsibility to her job, and feeling up Owen Gallagher was not part of it.

"I'm fine, Liz," Owen said softly. He reached out and wrapped his hand around her wrist. "Just a little embarrassed that I bit it like I did. I saw you walk out to your porch earlier so I figured you saw me fall. That's why I was lying down like I was. Not because I actually hurt, but because I'm an idiot."

She frowned, studying his face. "You're not an idiot. Everyone trips."

Owen rolled his eyes as he forced himself to a sitting position. She tried to help him, but he waved her off. "I trip more than others recently. Or, at least, it feels like that. Thanks for checking me out, though." He wiggled his brows. "And not just now."

She swore she could feel herself blush and she hated her pale skin. "Let's get you inside."

"Anything you say, Nurse Liz."

"And stop calling me that."

"But you *are* Nurse Liz," he said with a smile as they both stood up. "But I guess every time I call you that, I remind you that you *used* to be my nurse and that means it would be wrong to check out my butt. So I guess I'll stop doing that." He turned and shook his ass in her direction, looking over his shoulder as he did. "What do you think? You like the jeans? They're pretty old, but you should be able to get a nice glimpse of my assets."

She couldn't help herself.

She laughed and looked down at his butt. "Yes, I guess I can get a nice glimpse. But that's the only thing I'm getting. Just a glimpse."

"Whatever you say," Owen replied and took her hand. She was so surprised, she didn't pull away. "Can I offer you a cup of coffee? To say thanks for running to my aid?"

She thought of the bitter cup she'd left on her porch, but for some reason, she didn't answer as she should. "Okay."

Surprise filled his eyes for a moment, and it matched her own. "Okay." He smiled and pulled her toward his front door and inside. She hadn't gotten a good look at it last time, but now that she did, she liked what she saw. Strong lines and colors filled his home, and it looked like someone cleaned up daily.

In fact, she was pretty sure the place was cleaner than hers had ever been, and she *might* have been a little jealous of that fact.

"Cream and sugar?" Owen asked as he poured two cups.

"Both please," she said. "I can drink it black and usually do at work, but I have a sweet tooth."

Owen's eyes flared. "Good to know."

Liz licked her lips, and his eyes dropped down to follow the movement. This was so not a good idea. She shouldn't be here, and she sure as hell shouldn't be following up on any attraction they might share. He wasn't good for her, and she damn well knew she wasn't good for him.

And yet when he set her coffee cup next to her hand on the kitchen island, she didn't move to reach for it. Instead, she stood still, and he moved closer, so close she could feel his breath on her lips, the warmth of his body achingly close to hers.

"Tell me to stop," Owen whispered. He moved even closer, resting his hand on her hip. Her heart raced, and she tried to say no, tried to remember that she shouldn't do this.

She didn't tell him to stop.

He leaned forward, taking her mouth with his, and she let him. Let him have her, let him kiss her, let him do what she knew she shouldn't.

And she kissed him back.

It wasn't a soft kiss, wasn't one from fairy tales with fair maidens and handsome princes. Instead, it was a meeting of mouths, heavy breathing, teeth, and tongues fighting for control. He gripped her hip with one hand and dug the fingers of his other hand into her hair, pulling her impossibly closer.

She'd imagined his mouth on her lips, on her skin before, and yet those dreams had *nothing* on the real man. She wrapped her arms around him, needing him on her, *in* her, with her. When she found herself rocking against the hard length of him, she didn't stop. Instead, she just kissed him harder.

Owen's mouth was like nothing she'd had before, and she knew if she didn't stop soon she'd have sex with him right in his kitchen and not even care.

So it shouldn't have come as a surprise that it was *Owen* who stopped the kiss, pulling away with ragged breaths before resting his forehead on hers.

"Holy shit," he panted.

She couldn't say anything, could barely breathe herself.

"Don't say you regret that. Don't say we shouldn't have done it," Owen pleaded quickly. "If you don't know what to say, just don't say anything at all. But know that holy hell, woman, that kiss? That kiss was fucking everything. So if you're unsure about what to do next, you can walk away without saying a word. I totally get that because this was kind of a surprise. But, Liz? You walk away now without saying anything, you're telling me that I can find you again. Soon. So you make the choice. Just know that I want you. I fucking *want* you. But I won't take you, won't let you take me unless you want it. Got it?"

She swallowed hard, her breath finally calming.

And because she couldn't get him out of her head, couldn't stop thinking about what they'd just done, she turned and walked away.

But she didn't say anything.

That meant only one thing.

She *wanted* him to follow her. *Wanted* this to happen again.

She just hoped that she wasn't making the biggest mistake of her life.

Again.

"You're an idiot."

Owen glared at Murphy but didn't say anything. Instead, he took a sip of his beer and did his best to ignore his younger brother. They were supposed to be having a guys night in, where they didn't have to talk about anything important, and they could just watch whatever game was on TV, drink beer, eat things too greasy for men their age, and goof around.

Apparently, Murphy had other ideas.

"You're a little bit of an idiot," Jake put in from his side, and Owen held himself back from punching the guy. After all, his collarbone still hurt, and he didn't want to be called something worse than an idiot.

"So he tripped over his own two feet in the middle of his lawn while his hot neighbor watched, that doesn't make him *that* much of an idiot," Graham defended. Though Owen wasn't sure if that statement was truly a defense at all.

"I don't know why I told you guys that story," Owen grumbled.

"Because I caught the new bruise on your side when you reached up for the crackers," Murphy said. "I mean, seriously, if you're going to bruise yourself the minute we leave you alone, maybe you should come back and stay with one of us."

Owen flipped them off and took another sip of his

beer. "Shut up. I invited you guys over to watch the game, not piss me off."

"Pissing you off is a side benefit we all enjoy," Jake added lazily.

"And you still haven't told us what happened after Liz nursed you back to health after your fall." Owen glared at Graham for that statement and did his best to keep his expression neutral.

"You totally got some," Murphy said with a grin. "Maybe not all of it, but you got some of it."

Owen closed his eyes and counted to ten. Maybe when he opened his eyes, he'd have a new set of brothers that wouldn't annoy him as much. Fat chance.

"I'd say he at least kissed her," Jake said. "Not much else, though, or he'd be a shit ton more relaxed than he is now."

Graham chuckled. "Yeah, he's too grumpy to have that just lubed look."

"Fuck all of you."

"Yeah, just a taste, I think," Murphy said as if he were some wise man in the ways of women. "It's okay, bro. You still have time to make a move before she sees how boring you truly are and laughs you off."

"Again, fuck all of you." Owen chugged the rest of his beer and rolled to his feet off the couch, ignoring the aches and pains in his side. "I need another beer. You guys can get your own if you want more because I'm done with the lot of you. And when I get back, we're watching the damn game, and we're *not* talking about my fucking sex life anymore. Got me?"

"You say that as if you *have* a sex life," Jake said with a grin. "I mean, I know not everyone has the kind of sex life I have, but I would have thought you'd eventually get half of what I have."

Graham punched Jake in the shoulder, and Owen grinned. "Stop bragging," Graham grumbled. "But in reality, Blake is more than enough. No triads for me."

"Blake would probably cut anyone who got close to you to even angle for a triad," Murphy drawled.

"True enough," Graham said with a smile.

Owen just shook his head and went into the fridge to get four more beers. He might have said they could get their own, but he wasn't that much of an ass. For now anyway. If they kept talking about Owen's lack of sex life, he might just force them all to drink water and get out of his house early.

There was truly only so much teasing a man could take.

"So when do we get to meet this new client of ours?" Graham asked as Owen sank back down onto the couch, handing out the beers as he did.

Owen rubbed a hand over the scruff he should probably shave off soon for the next few meetings they had. While he liked his beard, ink, and piercings, not everyone they worked with wanted to see it all the time. His ink was easy to hide under clothes, and he always took out his brow ring for new clients. His other piercings were a little lower, so no one noticed them. As for the beard, he tried to shave it off every once in a while for certain clients that seemed to want a cleaner, fancier company representative to work with. Owen would do anything it took to get the job done, so he'd shave off the damn beard if he had to.

He'd just make sure he grew it out again when he went down on Liz. He had a feeling she'd like the scrape of his facial hair on her inner thighs as she rode his face.

Owen swallowed hard and did his best not to shift his position on the couch. No more thinking down *that* path tonight.

"Uh, probably in the next week or so. Since it's the whole street rather than a single project home, it's taking a bit to get things settled. It'll take the whole crew and then some to work on it in my estimation. Which is good because we have the opening coming up as long as we stay on schedule." They'd gotten off that schedule a bit with Owen's accident and Murphy's stitches, but they had all been working their asses off to make sure they kept their current clients happy.

"Well, I'm glad you're working on it since we've all been so busy," Murphy said as he took a bite of a chip with salsa. "Though this guy seems like he has a stick up his ass."

Owen didn't correct them. Clive Roland was a first-class asshole, who only liked the best of the best. It was Owen's job to show him that Gallagher Brothers Restoration was what he needed.

"The final paperwork should be signed within the next couple of weeks. Roland is just taking his sweet time with us."

Graham shook his head. "With Blake's family place in the books, we already have the high-end work we need. Anyone who sees the place after we worked on it should know what we can do. We got a few high-end clients after we finished it up, and people took notice. I don't know why this Roland guy is taking his time. If he doesn't think we're good enough now, then it's because he has an idea of perfection that doesn't exist. We're the best at what we do, and he should know it. If he doesn't, then we don't need him. We can find plenty of new jobs."

Owen bit his tongue so he wouldn't say something he didn't mean. This job wasn't just because Roland's company was one that could set the Gallaghers up for life. This was also one that Owen had been setting up himself because the others were busy. He needed this to work so he could show them that he could do more than organize their desks.

He didn't know why this one mattered more than the others in some respects, but he was going to do his best to make it work. As it was, they'd already had to turn down a couple of last-minute clients in preparation for Roland. If they didn't get this big job, they were going to be screwed in those months where they'd have to find new jobs for the company that might not exist. However, Owen didn't want to think about that now because he needed to remain positive. The job was almost complete in the books, and he would just have to work with that.

"We'll get this done," Owen said calmly. "We always do."

"Hell yeah, we do," Murphy said, ignoring the tension in the room. Or maybe his too-observant brother had caught on easily and wanted to move them in a new direction. Either way, Owen was grateful. "Hey, Jake, why isn't Border hanging out with us?"

Jake smiled before taking a sip of his drink. "It's Maya and Border's date night, and while I'd usually be hanging out at home with Noah while they go out, you guys wanted to do this instead."

"Hence why Blake is juggling Noah and Rowan

right now," Graham put in, though he grinned as he said it. "Rowan is trying to show us how good of a big sister she can be. I'm pretty sure she doesn't care if she gets a baby brother or sister as long as it's soon."

Owen studied his older brother's face. "So is it gonna be soon?"

Graham shrugged, but laughter danced in his eyes. "Maybe."

Murphy leaned forward with Jake. "Are we going to be uncles again?"

There was a casual seriousness in his tone that Owen felt, as well. The eldest Gallagher had been married once before and had also had a beautiful baby girl. When she'd died, Graham's marriage had fallen apart and so had Graham. The fact that he was now a loving father to Rowan and had even legally adopted her when he married Blake was a big thing. Now having him speak of a new baby was a *huge* thing, and Owen honestly couldn't be happier for his big brother. If anyone deserved that kind of happiness, it was Graham.

"Not yet," Graham answered. "We're still practicing."

Owen rolled his eyes, and the others laughed. "I'd have thought you guys would be worn out practicing by now," he added dryly.

"Never too much practicing," Graham said with a laugh.

Owen shook his head and leaned back into the couch as his brothers continued to joke around about making babies and other things he never would have thought they'd talk about as a group. The four of them had really started to grow up and reach the next level in recent years, and he couldn't help but feel a bit behind. He'd planned so much of his life, of his brothers' lives, and yet he didn't have a family to call his own.

Liz's face entered his mind, and he held back a frown. One kiss, one *very* hot and steamy kiss, did not make a relationship or a family. She was still too skittish around him, and he knew to even get her to go on a date with him was going to take a lot of work. But that's what Owen did. He planned and made things happen. Maybe with the right plan, the right list, he'd find a way into Liz's life and see what happened next.

That was if he could make the timing work. He still had his old clients, this new one, and the idea that someone out there had actually hit him with their car. It would all be a little too much for some people, but not Owen. He would make it work. And when he did, maybe, just maybe, he'd get to kiss Liz again.

He smiled into his beer as Jake and Murphy started yelling at each other and the TV. When Jake threw a fake punch at their little brother, Murphy tackled him to the ground. Owen took that time to make sure everyone's beer was firmly on a coaster and watched as Jake and Murphy wrestled on the floor the way they had for decades.

Some things might change in their lives, but not everything. They were Gallagher brothers through and through, after all.

Chapter Six

Liz wanted nothing more than to take a long bath before sleeping for the next fourteen hours, but she had a feeling that wouldn't be happening today. She'd worked an overnight shift since the administration office had been changing things around for the past month, and her body wasn't used to it yet. And she had a feeling by the time she did find a way to make it work mentally, they'd change her right back to days. Considering that had already happened twice, she knew she'd just have to live on coffee until the bosses figured out the budgets and how not to screw people around. People's lives depended on her, so yawning during an exam was out of the question.

She shuffled into the kitchen around noon and went straight for the coffee pot. She still needed to shower and do something about the rat's nest she called hair, but coffee was required first.

Tessa stood at the kitchen island, her jeans low on her hips as she danced to whatever song played on her headphones. She had a spoon in her hand, and her eyes were closed as she shimmied and shook, something halfway between cooking and whatever dance she called that movement.

Liz held back a smile as she went to her coffee, brushing by Tessa on the way. After her friend stopped screaming, Liz poured herself a cup and smiled.

"Good morning."

"Holy shit, woman," Tessa panted as she pulled her earbuds out of her ears. "Warn a bitch before scaring the shit of out her lurking around like that."

Liz flipped her friend off as she took a sip of the manna that would keep her looking alive the rest of the day. "I don't lurk."

"You sure as hell didn't make a sound when you came in."

She rolled her eyes. "You had your music up so loud, you wouldn't have heard me yell your name. Though I don't know why you had your eyes closed as you danced. Maybe to make sure you didn't have to see yourself, hmm?"

This time it was Tessa who flipped her off. "I hate

you, and I dance a hell of a lot better than you." She pointed at her hips. "These hips don't lie. I have moves. You amble and try to grind or whatever, even though you have way better curves than I do."

"I don't amble. Nor do I *try* to grind." Liz took another sip. "I grind just fine. Or at least I did when I actually danced."

Tessa rolled her eyes. "You need to start taking time for yourself or you're going to work yourself to the bone."

"It's not that bad," Liz argued. "Plus, we have to finish getting the house set up, and I haven't even *looked* at the yard. We're hitting the months where we need to start planning things for the spring now that the heavy snow has stopped."

"First, it's Denver, honey. The snow won't stop until June even though it'll fake us out for a month or so with hot weather. That's how it works here. As you've lived in this area your whole life, you know that. And second, you need to live beyond this house and your work. Shake your ass in public and drink a little too much."

"Are you saying I should go out dancing? Because I don't know of any places near here other than a few bars. And we aren't twenty-one anymore. We have responsibilities."

Tessa rolled her eyes. "Yeah, we do. And because we

do, we need to let off some steam. That's why today we're going over to Owen's house because Murphy invited us over."

"Why is Murphy inviting us over to Owen's house and not Owen?"

"Because Owen is throwing a party and wants us over there. Murphy just happened to be the one to call me."

Liz froze. She hadn't seen Owen since the kiss-that-shall-not-be-mentioned in his kitchen, and she wasn't sure she was ready to face him yet. Hell, she wasn't sure she'd ever be ready to face him. She could still feel the way his hand had gripped her hip, the way his tongue had dominated, the way his teeth had bit into her lip, making her want to climb up his body and never let go.

Tessa gave her a curious look, and Liz did her best not to press her thighs together since she knew she was already wet just thinking about Owen's mouth on her.

Damn Gallagher.

"What are you thinking about that's making your cheeks all red like that, hmm?" Tessa asked. "Because, honey, if it's making you look that embarrassed or turned on, I need details. And then you need to go finish what you started because I know you haven't been laid recently."

"Tessa!" Liz closed her eyes and pinched her nose.

"Stop doing that." Tessa had always been able to tell when Liz had finally had sex with the man she was dating, and she hated it. Not that she hated that Tessa knew, she didn't, but Liz hated that she could never tell with Tessa. Her friend was better at putting on a mask than anyone Liz knew.

"What? I'm just saying. And let me guess, it was Mr. Tall and Organized, right? Did Owen put his big hands on you?" Tessa's eyes danced as she finished mixing mustard into the potato salad Liz just now realized she'd been making. "How was it? No, don't tell me. I can totally guess from the way you want to kill me right now. He was hot, demanding, and ready to get you off right where you were. Only he didn't, because if he had, you'd be a lot more relaxed right now. So either something interrupted you or one of you ran. I'm going to say you because you're not talking about it and you look like you want to murder me right now."

Liz set down her empty coffee cup and took a deep breath. "I hate how you do that. You are totally in the wrong line of work. You could work for the police with the way you see things." She let out that breath. "Anyway, yes, Owen and I kissed. That was it. It was a mistake and won't be happening again."

"Why the hell not?" Tessa demanded as she put the potato salad into the fridge. "He's single. You're single.

You both give off those 'fuck me' vibes that only call to one another, and he's hot."

Liz rinsed out her cup and blew out a breath. "We don't give off those 'fuck me' vibes. And it's not like you've seen us together that much to know."

"I wasn't that drunk at the bar, Liz. I clearly remember the way you two kept looking at each other that night. Of course, you were glaring, and he was looking at you like a guppy in water, his mouth moving but no words coming out. Either way, though, I felt the flames. He's hot for you. You're hot for him. Just do him already."

"You're an idiot."

"No, I'm someone who likes sex. You used to be that person too until you started working as much as you do."

Liz glared. "You work as much as I do these days."

Tessa raised a brow. "Yeah, but I let off steam."

To the point sometimes it worried Liz, but she didn't say that. Tessa was her own person and could do what she needed to, but that didn't mean Liz wouldn't remain uncomfortable with some of it.

"He was a patient. His brother was a patient. I'm not going to sleep with him. Or Murphy."

Tessa snorted. "I know you're not going to sleep with Murphy. There wasn't chemistry there. But you and Owen?" She fanned her face. "Oh, Momma. But,

Liz darling, they were your patients for five minutes and never will be again. I know you. If for some reason they come into the ER again, you'll hand them over to another nurse. You wouldn't make things sticky."

"And if I do that, then Lisa and Nancy will have just one more reason to put me on edge since Lisa is fighting for the same position as me, and Nancy is in just as much trouble." Liz let her head fall back, her temples pounding. "How did I end up in high school again?"

"People are always going to act like they're fucking immature pricks who don't know how to deal with others. That's how life is. But you don't have to let them win. You're the best nurse there by far, and Lisa knows it. You're not going to lose your job because you happen to sleep with your neighbor. You're not his nurse anymore, and you will never treat him again in that hospital. If you're worried that it might get sticky that he's your neighbor, don't. We hardly ever see him, and the Gallaghers seem like nice people. They're not going to fuck us over."

Liz narrowed her eyes. "You say that, but I don't see you sleeping with Murphy." Liz hadn't missed the way the two of them flirted when they thought no one was watching...and even *when* they thought others were watching for that matter.

Tessa scoffed. "We're flirting because it's fun. But

I'm not as sex-deprived as you, and I don't know if I want to sleep with Murphy. I like him as a friend. And you know how I tend to fuck things up once I sleep with a guy."

"Then why do you think it's okay for me to sleep with Owen?"

"Because things are different. *You're* different. And hell, you've already kissed him. Just make it happen and stop overthinking it. You're stressing me out."

"You can't just push me into having sex with a guy so I'll stop stressing you out."

Tessa rolled her eyes. "No, I can't. And I'm not. I'm pushing the other shit out of your way so you can do what you want to and not freak yourself out about it. If you want to sleep with him, date him, pour hot wax on him after you tie him to the bed, go for it. Just don't stay away because you're scared. You need to live a little, Liz. It's okay to do that."

"Hot wax?" Liz asked, pointedly ignoring the rest of Tessa's statement.

"I don't know your kinks. I mean, I know some of them since the walls have been pretty thin in our apartments, but the hot wax thing might be a secret fetish." She grinned, and Liz threw the dishrag at her.

"I hate you."

"No, you don't. You love me. Now go shower and

put on those skinny jeans I bought you. You're going to look hot as fuck and maybe get fucked."

"One, you're crude when you're pushy. Two, I'm not going to fit my very large ass into those jeans. I don't know why you bought them for me."

Tessa just used the dishrag to clean up the mess from the potato salad mixings. "You love me. And all you need to do is lay down on the bed and wiggle them on. I'll help you if you need it, but your ass looks freaking amazing in them. Owen won't be able to stop looking at it." She frowned. "Though maybe you should wear another pair because they'll probably be hard to get off in a hurry. Though he could like that, you know. The ripping and tugging as you guys are all panting and trying to get to each other's private parts."

Liz held up a hand. "Please, stop talking. I beg you."

Tessa grinned. "You love me," she repeated. "Now shower, get dressed, and actually brush your hair. Then we're heading over to Owen's. The Gallaghers will all be there, and they want us over there."

"Murphy wants us there," Liz corrected. "We don't know about the others."

"Get a move on!"

With a sigh, she went back to her bedroom and pulled out the jeans she didn't think she'd actually fit in. She would *not* be sleeping with Owen tonight, and not ever for that matter. Maybe wearing jeans that were hard to get out of would ensure that she stuck to that.

Hopefully.

"You made it!" Murphy said as he opened Owen's front door. She knew the man didn't actually live here, but he sure acted like it. "I was afraid Tessa wouldn't be able to convince you to come."

Tessa hip-bumped her as she handed over the potato salad to the large Gallagher at the door. "Of course, I convinced her. I'm good at convincing people to do all manner of things."

Murphy winked at Tessa, and Liz wanted to bang her head on the doorframe. And people thought Liz and Owen flirted. Holy hell.

"Good to know, Tessa. Good to fucking know."

Liz cleared her throat, and Murphy turned to her, his smile in place. Nothing seemed to faze him, and she kind of liked that.

"Come on in," Murphy said as he moved out of the way. "Everyone is in the back since Owen had us put those built-in heaters out there. It's not too chilly but with him still being on the mend and Rowan wanting to play outside, we wanted to be careful. I'll go put the salad in the fridge since we're still working on cheese and veggies and things. Drinks are outside so make sure the crew shows you where they are." He hurried off, and Liz watched as Tessa followed his movements.

"Are you sure you don't want to bang him?" Liz whispered.

"Who has the dirty mouth now?" Tessa asked with a laugh. "And as much as I love watching that man move, I'm having more fun flirting." She held up a hand before they made their way to the back of the house where the French doors led to the patio. "It's not the same as you and Owen. I've already gone over this. Now put a smile on your face and be prepared to have fun. You need it."

"I don't know how you convinced me to show up here when I have so many things to do at the house. Plus, I can't drink since I'm on-call tonight. *And* I don't know how I ended up in these jeans. I can barely breathe in them."

"I can barely breathe watching you walk in them."

Liz froze at the sound of Owen's voice, and Tessa grinned. "Hey, Owen. Thanks for inviting us."

Liz turned, her body on fire from Owen's mere presence alone.

"Thanks for coming," Owen said, his eyes on Liz and not on Tessa.

"Come on, Tessa," Murphy put in as he shuffled past them. "I think I see a drink with your name on it."

"Hell, yeah," Tessa said as she pushed past Liz. "Have fun, you two!"

With that, the French doors slammed shut, and Liz was left alone in a hallway with the man she'd told herself she would stay away from. From where they stood, no one could see them, and Owen's doors seemed to be thick enough that she couldn't hear a thing going on outside. It was as if they were the only two people in the world, and she didn't know what to do about that. She hadn't even said hello to the other guests, and yet, the only thing she wanted to do was move closer to this particular Gallagher.

"So...Murphy invited us. I hope that's okay."

Owen took one step forward, the heat of him so close she knew she'd singe if she touched him. "Murphy seems to have ideas about us, and I wasn't going to stop him from asking you and Tessa over."

He reached up and tucked a piece of her hair behind her ear, and she licked her suddenly dry lips. How could this man do that to her? She didn't even know him, and yet she wanted to, wanted to know the feel of him, the way he tasted, the way he moved.

"Where is your sling?" she asked, her voice annoyingly breathy. "Shouldn't you be taking it easy?"

His finger traced her jaw, and her breath caught. "I'm allowed to move without it. I'm almost fully healed as it is other than the road rash and some aches and pains. And as for taking it easy, I'm pretty sure you'll be the judge of that, don't you think?"

She blinked, unaware that he'd moved closer, their hips now brushing, the long, thick, line of his cock pressing against her belly.

Holy hell. She was in over her head, and yet she wasn't sure she cared.

"What are we doing?"

He cupped her face, his head lowering. "I don't know, Liz. I don't fucking know."

When his lips touched hers, her eyes closed, and her mouth parted. He tasted of soda and Owen, sweet and salty. She wanted to devour him, but with the way *he* kissed *her,* she knew it would be the other way around.

Before she could think, he'd pulled her toward the open door behind them and had her back pressed to the other side of it, his hands on her body, her hands on his back. The quick snap of the lock told her he'd locked them into the room, and she couldn't focus on that. Instead, she slid her hands up his back, under the thin knit of his sweater, and moaned into him. His skin was so hot, so soft, and yet she wanted *more.*

Owen pulled away, his breath coming in pants as he reached under her shirt, cupping her breasts over her bra. "You're so fucking sexy, Liz. Did you think about what you were going to do to me when you showed up in those jeans? I want to pull them down ever so slightly so I can cup that thick ass of yours as I fuck you. Are you going to let me do that? Are you going to let me sink my cock into that pussy so we both can come hard against this door?"

She shuddered in his hold, gasping as he pinched her nipple. "We shouldn't."

His eyes darkened. "Tell me why."

"Because...because..." Well, hell, she couldn't think of a good reason right then. "We're neighbors!" she blurted. "It would make things complicated."

He licked her lip before biting down. "We can make sure we don't complicate things. I like you, Liz. I want to get to know you. I want to *feel* you."

"You say that, but people always complicate things. It's how it works."

He bit her earlobe, and her legs went weak. "Then we'll be careful. Kiss me, Liz. Kiss me back."

And because she was weak, she kissed him back. Her hands slid up his back again, her body shaking as he molded and cupped her breasts. When she tilted her head back, he latched on to her neck, kissing and licking until she was on the edge of coming already, and he hadn't even touched her core.

As soon as she thought that, he had his hand on the

button of her jeans, trying to work them off. "These are fucking tight, babe. No wonder you look hot as fuck in them."

She groaned and reached out to cup him through his jeans. When he hissed out a breath, he grinned. "I wore them on purpose you know."

"To fuck with me?" he groaned, pumping into her hand.

"Maybe...but more to make sure I kept them on with you around."

His eyes darkened. "That's not going to work, babe. I'm going to tear these off if I have to. But the idea that you thought tight pants would keep me from wanting to fuck you? Honey, you have no idea."

She leaned forward and bit his lip. "Does it help you to know that I want you to fuck me? That *your* jeans cup your ass so well that I'm going to have visions of your thick thighs and cock for weeks to come?"

Liz wasn't averse to dirty talk, but her previous lovers hadn't really wanted her to speak during sex. Owen, however, groaned and tugged a belt loop on her jeans.

"Keep talking like that, and I'm going to end up dry humping you against the fucking door."

She laughed, revved up and not even embarrassed. She might have reservations, and knew this was probably a mistake, but she couldn't care right then. Like all things that worried her, she'd deal with it later.

He slid his hand between her legs and used the seam of her jeans to press against her clit. "Help me take down these jeans, Lizzie. I don't want to hurt you."

"Only if you do the same," she breathed.

He smiled then, looking even sexier than before, and nodded. "Deal. I like the way you think." He pulled away to undo the zipper on her jeans while she worked on his. They wiggled and grunted, shifting to pull down their pants just below their hips. It probably wasn't the sexiest looking thing in the world, but hell, she had never been more turned on.

She froze as she caught sight of his cock. "Holy hell. You're pierced?"

Owen played with the tip of his dick, rubbing his fingers over the two metal bars. "It's a dydoe piercing. Is that going to be a problem? I can take them out right now if you want."

She shook her head, her gaze on his cock. "I want to know what that feels like in me."

She looked up as Owen smiled widely. The light coming from beneath the blinds on the window behind them not only glinted on his brow ring, but the metal on his dick, as well. She'd never known she wanted a man so pierced, but hell, now she needed to know what she'd been missing.

"Since I'm guessing you've never had a man with them before, I'll be careful. I have condoms that work well over them and don't split. But if you were going down on me, I'd take them out the first time to protect your teeth."

She licked her lips, imagining his cock sliding down her throat as she teased him. "Okay." She wasn't sure she had enough brain cells right then to think of something else.

Owen reached between them again, and she let out a whine. "You're so fucking wet for me," Owen growled. "I can see the spot on your panties." He pressed his knuckle over the damp cotton, and she panted. "You're going to make me come just by looking at you." He tugged her panties out of the way and speared her with two fingers before she could respond. He had one hand on her neck, keeping her in place, and he kissed her brutally. Her body shook. She reached between them and grasped his cock, using the semen dripping at the tip to keep from rubbing him too hard.

Their bodies close together, their mouths never leaving each other, she jerked him off, her hand not quite big enough to reach fully around him while he fucked her hard with his hand. With each movement, her back slammed against the door, the sound echoing in the small room. She knew anyone standing outside it would know what they were doing, and she didn't care. She just wanted Owen.

When his thumb pressed firmly against her clit, she came, her eyes rolling back, and her hips unabashedly riding his hand. She kept her grip on his dick, needing him to come with her, but he pulled away at the last moment, his body shaking.

"I need to come inside you, not on your belly." He kissed her, this time softer, as if he couldn't get enough of her. "Let me get the condom from the dresser. Don't move."

She was still shaking from her orgasm, but didn't know what to think, she just needed *him*. He left her standing there, her jeans still high up on her legs and her shirt rucked up so the undersides of her breasts were bare. She knew she could fix herself, make it look as if she weren't so wanton, but she didn't care. Instead, she slid her hand between her legs to play with herself, wanting to be near the edge again. If Owen didn't like it, well, he could just get himself off.

When he turned, back, his cock slapping his belly since he'd stripped off the rest of his clothes at some point, he froze.

"You have got to be the sexiest fucking woman I've

ever seen in my life," he panted. "Do you make yourself come a lot? Are you thinking of me right now?" He gripped the base of his cock as he slid the condom on, his eyes never leaving hers. "That's it, Lizzie. Slide those fingers through your wet folds."

"Owen," she breathed, her hand moving slowly. "I need you."

"You need me, Lizzie? Need my cock?" He bit down on his lip as he cupped his balls.

"Get in me already before I make myself come," she ordered, and he smiled widely.

"Well, since you asked so nicely." He moved to her quickly and cupped her face with one hand, the other coming over hers to help her get off. He kissed her quickly, their tongues tangling as he rocked his cock against her. "You taste so fucking good. And next time, I'm going to see how you taste between your thighs. I'd do it right now, but I can't wait. I'm sorry for being so selfish."

Next time?

She pulled away, panting. "You got me off, and I haven't been able to reciprocate. That's not selfish."

He grinned, and she let out a breath. He was so freaking beautiful it wasn't fair. "Turn around for me."

She raised a brow. "Excuse me."

"I told you that I wanted to fuck you in those jeans.

You going to let me?"

Liz smiled, her heart racing. "Oh, yeah. I forgot."

"Orgasms can do that to a person." He slapped her ass as she turned, and she let out a moan. "Oh, yeah, your ass is so fucking sexy in these jeans when you have them on, but rucked up right under your butt like this? I'm going to come just looking."

She looked over her shoulder as she pressed her hands to the wood of the door. "No fucking my actual ass, Owen. Not on the first date." She winked as she said it, and his eyes widened. She watched as he gripped the base of his cock, squeezing so tightly she knew he was on the verge of coming.

"I think you're my new favorite person. Ever." He pressed closer, his cock sliding between her cheeks before going lower. "I won't even touch you there with my fingers this time." He paused. "Okay, fine, maybe my fingers if I can't help myself and you're into it. But no butt sex our first time. That I can promise."

She laughed, unaware that she could laugh when she was so horny. Owen did things to her she couldn't explain, and yet she wanted more of it. He made her laugh, made her think, made her angry, and yes, made her want to come more than she'd ever wanted to before. He was a complicated man, and she knew that was dangerous, but right then, she couldn't care.

She just *needed* him.

He hovered over her, his front to her back, and he took her mouth, her head over her shoulder. She arched into him, and his cock slid even closer, the tip playing dangerously with her folds. She could feel the piercing beneath the condom, and just the thought of it pushed her even closer

"Fuck me, Owen. Please."

He bit her lip. Hard. "As you wish." He slammed into her in the next instant, and they both called out, freezing as he got to the root.

"Holy hell."

She wasn't sure which of them had said it, but she had a feeling it was both of them.

"You're so fucking tight, Liz. I'm not going to last long."

She reached behind her and gripped his ass, her nails digging in. "I don't care. Just make me come."

He let out a rough laugh before starting to move. She pressed back into him with every thrust, meeting his flesh, her ass pressed against his hips. He was so big that he stretched her, filling her up until she could barely breathe, but she didn't care.

When he slid one hand around her to rub her clit, she came, her inner walls tightening around him. He captured her lips and her scream as he came with her, his body pumping, the warmth of him creating an inferno between them.

And as he slowed his movements, both their bodies shaking, he kissed up her neck and toward her mouth, sweetly, caringly, as if they hadn't just fucked like animals against the door.

"I..." he trailed off, and she let out a breath. Not knowing what to say either.

"Hey, you two. If you're done, you might want to clean up. Graham is about to start cooking the meat." Murphy laughed on the other side of the door, and Liz froze. "Of course, it sounds like you two have all the meat you need."

"You're an idiot," Tessa called out, and Liz closed her eyes, mortified. "Don't worry, though all the adults knew what you two were up to, only Murphy and I heard the end. Good job, Owen! She needed that."

"I'm going to kill you!" Liz called back.

Owen was still buried balls-deep inside her, and was currently laughing against her skin. If she weren't equally turned on, sated, and embarrassed at the same time, she might have laughed with him.

"You love me," Tessa called out. "But I think you like riding Owen's dick more."

"Murphy," Owen said, his voice low.

"I'm on it," the younger Gallagher said slowly.

"Come on, Tessa. Let's go outside and give them a minute to clean up. Don't be too long, you two. Blake and Maya will be in next, and compared to them, we're the gentle ones."

Liz hit her head against the door as Owen kissed behind her ear. She hated herself for shivering in delight but leaned into him when he kissed her again.

"I can't believe I just had sex with you with your family right outside."

Owen pulled out of her, and she winced. When he turned her around and cupped her face, kissing her softly, she leaned into him. "I honestly can't believe it either, *but* only Tessa and Murphy heard, and if they had heard more than the tail end of it, they'd have said something. Every single adult outside has had sex before, Liz. It's okay that we did this. It's *really* okay. We just couldn't wait, and yeah, I'll get ribbed for it, but I'm always getting ribbed for something."

Liz kept her eyes closed. "But they have *kids* out there."

"Who didn't hear or see anything and were most likely kept distracted by sugar. Now let me get us cleaned up and take care of the condom. Then we'll go out there, get a drink and a burger, and enjoy the rest of the evening. Okay?" He kissed her again, and this time when he pulled back, she opened her eyes. "Don't regret this, Liz. Don't pull away because you're embarrassed. I'll kick their asses if they make you feel like what we did was wrong."

She pressed her lips together and did her best not to say something she would regret but she knew it was too late. He'd seen it in her eyes. He let his hands fall and took a step back.

"I see."

She shook her head. "No, you don't see. Because I don't. I just...this was fast for me, Owen. I need time to think." She pulled up her jeans, wincing at how sore she knew she'd be later. "I'm going home. I'm not running from you, but from them. I don't want it to be awkward."

Owen shook his head. "It'll be more awkward now, but I'm not going to make you do anything you don't want to do." He leaned forward as if to kiss her, then thought better of it. "Find me when you're ready to talk." And with that, he walked back to the bathroom attached to his room, and Liz pulled down her shirt.

She knew she was being an idiot and making a mistake, but she couldn't think. She needed space to process what had just happened, and sitting with his family wasn't going to help that.

She just hoped that when she figured it out, Owen wouldn't hate her for it.

Chapter Seven

Well, it was official, Owen was a fucking idiot. He was pretty sure he'd said those exact words to himself concerning a certain blonde next door before, but it didn't change the fact that he was well and truly fucked.

He shouldn't have moved as fast as he had, and they both knew it. It had only been two days since he'd had Liz's body wrapped around him as he'd made her come with his fingers before pressing her pretty breasts to the door so he could fuck her from behind. He'd never done or seen anything as erotic as her in the throes of passion, and yet he knew they shouldn't have gone that far, that fast.

If they'd merely kissed, he knew there wouldn't be this awkwardness between them—or at least this level of it. Instead, she'd run right out of his home before he could even tuck his dick back into his pants—if he had been wearing any. Every single adult in his backyard had known what happened and had given him either humorous looks or ones of accusation. It wasn't as if he'd been alone in the mauling. She'd had her hands on him just the same and hadn't been able to deal with it.

He wasn't doing much better, though.

Owen couldn't get over how she'd felt beneath his touch, and how much she'd pushed at him to do the same things to him as he was doing to her.

She'd said she hadn't run because of him but because of their audience, and as much as he wanted to believe that, he couldn't quite do so. She'd told him they'd moved too fast, and he agreed since this was the outcome, but he didn't regret their time together. There was no way he could ever taint that heat, that hunger, with regrets.

But no matter what happened next, she would have to make the next move. He wouldn't risk himself like that again, because despite what others may think, he had feelings. He wasn't a drone behind a desk, wasn't a robot who simply got through the workday.

He was a damn man and wasn't about to push Liz too hard because he was careless.

When she was ready—if she were ever ready—she'd

come to him, and then they'd see what the next step was. Owen honestly had no idea if she would make that choice, and hell, he had no clue about the next step either. For all his planning and organizational skills, he'd never thought to plan for this and didn't know where to begin.

While part of him hadn't wanted to let her go, he knew that forcing the issue would have been a mistake. So now, here he was, on a weekend where in the past he'd have been at the worksite getting things prepped for Monday, sitting around with this thumb up his ass. There had to be a better way to spend his time other than ruminating on what had happened with Liz.

With a frown, he pulled out his phone and scrolled through his house chore list. There were a few deep cleaning things he could start since spring was on its way, but he wasn't in the mood to begin that. Plus, though he was almost up to a hundred percent from the accident, he wasn't sure that bending and doing a heavy cleaning would be the best idea for him.

He had a few shopping items on his list, but that didn't sound interesting at the moment either. When he got to the next thing, he gave a small nod. Outdoor work would be just the thing. He'd be able to breathe in the clean, mountain air, enjoy the sun on his face since they were hitting the time of year when it could be warm, hot, cold, and cool all in one day, and get his lawn and garden ready for the spring and summer.

While he wasn't the greenest thumb in the world, he wasn't too bad at it. All it took was research and practice to get some semblance of a yard that could almost take care of itself. At least, that's what he told himself. He'd only killed a couple of plants that first year, but he'd been an idiot and had listened to the wrong person about installation instead of doing the research himself. As much as some people touted experience and knowledge, Owen knew he could only take some of it at face value. Research and careful organization were the only ways to make things work in his mind.

With a sigh, he put away his phone before going back into his bedroom to change into outdoor clothes he wouldn't mind getting dirt on. While he sometimes wore suits or at least nicer clothes than his brothers for his job since he met with the clients more often than they did, he still owned more than his fair share of jeans and t-shirts that bore holes and stains from working on the jobsite. Before his accident, at least half of his days were spent working side by side with the crew, sweat and dirt dripping off them as they laid tile or put up drywall. Hopefully, soon, he'd be able to get back to it since he was almost fully healed. He'd just have to get past his brothers, and that didn't sound like it was going to be easy. And while he couldn't fully blame them since he'd have done the same—and *had* in some cases—if any of them were in his position, he still resented it. He wanted to get back to work as if nothing had happened; like he hadn't been hit by a damn truck in a parking lot.

He shook those thoughts off like he always did and quickly got dressed, picking up his phone again on his way out the back door. He did his best not to think about Liz pressed up against him in his bedroom since those thoughts wouldn't be helping him today, but it wasn't easy.

Deciding to work on the front of the house first, he picked up his tools from his custom shed out back and lumbered his way to the front. While the back yard had more things to do, the front yard held the sun this morning, and it was the first thing people saw when they walked up. He might as well make that look like he cared since he was out here.

It took all his strength not to look over at his neighbor's and see if Liz's vehicle was in the driveway. Neither she nor Tessa seemed to want to park in the two-car garage, but he had a feeling it was because that's where they currently stored some of the boxes they hadn't yet unpacked. It would annoy him to no end to have things left undone like that, and knew it annoyed

Liz to some degree. She and Tessa were both take-charge women—a trait he admired—but they also worked even longer hours than he did. Between work, getting parts of the house fixed up, and needing to sleep, Owen didn't know how the two of them had any energy at all left at the end of the day.

No wonder Liz wanted nothing to do with him.

He closed his eyes and let out a small growl. Hell, he was out here on his hands and knees, digging up the front bed for the spring so he wouldn't think about her, and yet all he'd done so far was exactly that. There was a reason Owen usually ended up sleeping with women who had nothing to do with the other parts of his life and fit neatly into boxes. They were always casual, put together, and would end up walking away sated but not hurt when Owen wanted to move on. That made him sound like an ass, though, so he once again pushed those thoughts from his brain.

Resigned, he dug into the older mulch and cleaned up leaves that he'd missed the previous fall, as well as any weeds that dared to show their faces. He had a few bags of the new mulch in the shed out back, and would use the wheelbarrow to get them out instead of just carrying them on his shoulder like usual. He might be healing, but he wasn't stupid. There was no way he wanted to push back his recovery just so he could prove himself.

"Fuck me."

His head turned so fast he almost made himself dizzy. Liz stood with her hands on her hips as she glared at a yellow bush in front of her house. And since he happened to know that the bush should be green all year round, he had a feeling the poor thing had seen the last of its days.

After wiping his hands on his jeans, he stood up and made his way over to Liz, knowing he was taking his life in his hands. He might have said he'd stay away from her sexually, but she was his neighbor, and being helpful came with the job.

Sure, Owen, keep telling yourself that.

"Fuck me," she repeated, and his dick went on alert.

Down, boy.

"I'd say I'd help, but I'm pretty sure we already covered that."

Smooth, Owen. Smooth.

She turned and glared at him, her cheeks going slightly pink. From embarrassment or arousal, he didn't know, but damn if he didn't wish it were the latter.

"I didn't know anyone was out here."

He tilted his head over at his lawn. "I was on my

knees over there, working on the front bed, so you probably didn't see me when you looked out." And at the mention of knees, an image of Liz on her knees in front of him while she sucked him off filled his brain, and he did his best to push it away. Holy hell, that was one image he wanted to make real, but only if she came to him first.

Only then.

He wouldn't push her, not again, but damn it, he wanted her, and not just for that smoking body of hers.

Danger, Owen Gallagher, danger.

Sometimes, his brain was a little off-kilter.

"Well, I'm sorry my outburst distracted you," Liz said after a moment, her eyes darkening the longer the two of them stared at each other. He'd done his best to keep a reasonable distance between them, but it would only take one step, one touch of skin against skin to have them practically on top of one another.

"You didn't," he said with a shrug. "I'm just working slowly since I was bored as hell in my house." He nodded toward the plant. "Having an issue?"

She narrowed her eyes. "It's fine."

He gave the yellow plant a sad look. "It's dead."

She huffed out a breath. "It can't be. We just moved in. I can't have killed a plant after *just* moving in. It's not possible."

He stuffed his hands in his pockets so he wouldn't

make a mistake and touch her. "It could have been on its way out before you moved in. Plants die for all sorts of reasons, and the people renting the house before you didn't really take care of anything."

She closed her eyes and groaned. "I know. That's why Tessa and I bought the house for what we did. The previous tenants, and probably the tenants before them, treated the house like shit. The plan was for Tessa and me to clean it up and upgrade it over time, but it's looking to be more of a challenge than we'd thought considering plants are outright committing suicide before I even get a chance to figure out how to take care of them."

Hell, she and Tessa had even more on their plate than he'd thought. And though he'd soon be working all hours of the night on the new project, he knew he couldn't just stay away.

"You do realize that my brothers and I own a business that deals with all of this, right? We can help."

Her eyes flared, and he knew he'd said the wrong thing. "We can do it on our own. We always have."

"But that doesn't mean you have to."

"I'm not paying you to do something we can do, Owen."

He narrowed his eyes. "I didn't mention compensation."

Now she looked even angrier. "And I'm not getting the work done for free, damn it. What kind of woman do you think I am?"

"You said you weren't getting the work done at all. And there are other ways to pay for help."

He should have expected the punch to the gut, only it took more wind out of him than he'd expected.

"Shit! I forgot. Oh my God. I've never hit anyone in my life, and I just hit a man with an open wound."

Owen waved her off, and she tugged at his shirt. His breathing was a little better now. "I'm not bleeding or anything. And you hit the other side of my body where there wasn't bruising and where there hadn't been an incision. I'm fine, and from the way my words sounded, I totally deserved it."

"I *hit* you." Her eyes were wide, her face pale, and he took her hands in his, stopping her from pulling his shirt off in broad daylight.

"And if you thought I was talking about payment with your body, then I deserved it. I was actually saying that we could trade off on things, or give you a discount since you're my neighbor. Or even just find a way to make it work by *showing* you how to do things so you can do it yourself. I know you're independent, Liz, and I wouldn't ever take that away from you."

She still looked too pale, and he wasn't sure if she

understood what he was trying to say. He hated that he'd said what he did that way, and though his side wasn't hurting from her fairly weak punch, he probably should have been hit harder.

"Come inside with me and let me check you out."

He raised a brow but didn't say anything as she pulled him into her house. He was really okay, but if she was that worried, he wasn't going to stop her, not when it meant that he got to have her hands on him.

He really was a bastard sometimes.

"Shirt off," she said when they'd made it into her kitchen. The place needed a new coat of paint, some patch-up work, and probably a brand new kitchen after someone gutted it, but Liz and Tessa had put a sense of home into what they'd unpacked so far. If Liz gave him the go ahead, he knew he and his brothers could help her make this place a true home that she could be proud of. Only she was so independent, he wasn't sure that was ever going to work, not with the way she kept pushing him away.

Of course, now that he was shirtless in her kitchen with her hands roaming over his side, he didn't feel very pushed away at all. In fact, from the way his cock was pushing at the zipper of his jeans, he felt *very* near to her. *Very.*

"Your bruises and road rash are clearing up nicely,"

she said, her voice low and so not like how she'd been when she was on duty. Their proximity had to be getting to her, as well.

"I told you that you didn't hit me that hard," he said softly, putting his hand over hers. "I'm okay, Liz. I deserved the punch for the way my words sounded."

She finally looked up into his eyes and pressed her lips together. "I still shouldn't have hit you. I'm a healer. Not someone who lashes out."

Knowing he might be doing something stupid, he cupped her face with his hand and licked his lips. "You need to relieve the pressure sometimes, babe. We all do."

Her mouth parted, and she let out a shaky breath. If he weren't already hard as a rock, then the sight of her just now would have sent him straight there.

"What are you doing to me?" she breathed. "I shouldn't be doing this. I should be staying away and working on myself. Not getting caught up with you."

His thumb brushed along her cheekbone. "Why not get caught up with me?"

"Because I shouldn't."

"Do you always do things you should?"

Her hand slid down his bare chest, her skin soft and sending shocks straight down to his dick. "Usually, but there really isn't anything usual about you is there, Owen Gallagher?"

His mouth quirked into a grin. "Maybe. But you'll have to get closer to find out."

She leaned forward then, her hand on the edge of his jeans tightening. She brushed her lips against his. She had been the one to make a move, and for that he was grateful. Now if only she would move a bit farther south, then he could be sure that he wasn't the one pushing too hard.

She tasted of coffee and sugar, and he knew he could drown in her if he weren't careful. The kiss might have started out hesitant, but it was anything but by the time she pulled away, going to her knees in front of him.

"You don't have to. Not this time. Your knees are going to get hurt on the tile." He ran his hand through her long, blonde hair as she undid the button on his jeans before slowly unzipping him.

"I want to. And don't worry about my knees, Owen. Just worry about what I'm going to do with your cock."

His eyes widened at that statement before crossing. She rubbed her hand over him through his boxer briefs, a little smile playing on her face. Damn, he wanted to know what she was thinking just then, but all thoughts flew from his mind as she kissed the tip of him through the cotton.

"I love that you can feel the piercing through your underwear," she said softly before looking up. She was a fucking naughty angel on her knees, and he knew he'd have to be careful before he blew his load too early. "Of course, I also loved the feeling of your piercing inside me when you were fucking me. So, apparently, I have a thing for it."

His hand tightened in her hair. "Oh, yeah?"

She licked her lips. "Yeah. And the ink on your side? I love it. I'm so glad the incision didn't touch it, and the bruising is lightening up so I can see more of it. Oh, and the way you raise your brow and the ring looks all sexy? I could totally get off on that. Just saying."

Owen swallowed hard, trying to control himself. While he liked talking dirty in bed—or in the kitchen this time—he'd never been with a woman who liked talking dirty back. He'd been missing out because, *holy fuck.*

"I love your mouth," he said suddenly. "Not just because it's really close to my dick, but because I love the things you say. You could probably get me off just from your words alone."

"Ditto, Owen. Oh so ditto." Then she reached in and pulled him out so she could lick the tip.

"Fuck." He took a deep breath and gripped the base of his cock before pulling away. "I need to take out the piercings if you're going to suck me off, babe. I don't want to hurt your teeth."

She shook her head. "As long as you stay still and don't fuck my face, I'll be careful. I promise."

His knees shook like a schoolgirl's, but he leaned against the kitchen island so he wouldn't be tempted to thrust in and out of her mouth. He refused to hurt her, and if she wanted to lick him up like a Popsicle, then he wasn't going to stand in her way.

She licked up the side of him, one hand over his at the base while the other cupped his balls. His back tingled, as she squeezed and sucked, taking her time over the tip so she didn't bang the piercings against her teeth. His breath came in pants, and she sucked more of him into her mouth, her tongue doing wicked things to the underside of his dick. When she pulled away, he used his other hand to play with her hair, careful not to thrust inside her mouth, but damn it, he was too close to the edge.

She played with him longer, licking and sucking, his body sweating at the exertion it took not to move, but he couldn't take it any longer. When she pulled away to breathe, he backed up and reached down to grip under her arms so she stood in front of him.

"I wasn't done."

He kissed her hard before pulling back. "And I need to taste you." He toed off his shoes and pants before lifting her into his arms, keeping his mouth on hers. She wrapped her legs around him, her jeans pressing over his dick, and he shuddered a breath, knowing he needed to be inside her soon or he'd blow too quickly. "Bedroom?"

She pointed behind her. "Last one on the left."

"My left or yours?" he asked with a grin, kissing up her jaw.

"Yours. Now move quickly. I want that mouth on me."

He kissed her hard and did as she asked before depositing her on the bed, taking note of the nearly unpacked room. He'd care about her furniture and the colors later. Right then, he needed his head between her thighs.

"You say the sexiest things," he replied before kneeling between her legs. He somehow tugged her jeans off as well as her shoes before pulling at her panties. He quickly got them both all the way naked so there wouldn't be any obstacles later. He even tugged the condom out of his pocket he knew was still good since he'd checked on it after he slept with her the first time.

"Gotta love when you wear cotton," he breathed, his hands sliding up her thighs. "Keeps you all nice and soft for me."

She blushed, pressing her knees together. "I didn't expect this, or I'd have worn something sexier."

"Nothing sexier than you spread before me," he said honestly. "Now keep those knees up by your head, Lizzie. I'm going to eat this cunt of yours until you come on my face. How does that sound?"

She didn't blush this time. Instead, she gripped her knees with her hands and spreading herself for him. "Eat away, Gallagher. Let's see what you've got."

Holy hell, he was in for it with this one. "One thing you have to know about me, Liz."

"Hmm?" she asked, one brow raised.

"I *love* eating a woman out. Fucking love it."

She smiled like a cat in cream. "Good, because if you love it that much, you should be good at it. Be a good boy, Gallagher, and make me come."

He laughed, loving the blunt way she spoke, before gripping the backs of her thighs and lowering his face. He hadn't lied about his love for eating pussy. He craved it, needing the taste on his tongue. There was nothing like going down on a woman, knowing she would come right there because *you* were the one giving her pleasure. Yeah, he loved sex, too, especially when she squeezed his dick dry, but going down on a woman was even better. He got to be the one in control, got to be the one tasting, licking, touching, searching for just the right spot deep inside her that he could play with until she came with a rush. He'd be harder than steel by the end of it, and then he could pump inside her swollen flesh until they both came together.

Seriously, oral was the best thing ever.

He licked up her slit, loving the way she was already wet for him. His hands massaged the backs of her thighs as he licked and sucked. Her clit was already swollen and peeking out of the hood, so he sucked on that, too. She called out his name and tried to squirm, but with his hold on her, she couldn't move away. Instead, he flicked his tongue over her clit until she panted before sucking her lower lips into his mouth one at a time, exploring the undersides with his tongue. She tasted so damn good, and he knew this one time would never be enough.

"Hold yourself up, Lizzie," he growled, pressing kisses to each of her inner thighs. "I'm going to need my hands for this."

"Ugh...er..."

Apparently, she was at a loss for words, and he couldn't help but feel a bit smug at that.

He spread her with one hand before dipping his tongue deep inside her. She bucked toward him, and he bit down on her inner thigh.

"Stay still, babe." An order.

"I can't." A breath.

"I know." A growl.

He speared her with three fingers, curling them up to find her g-spot. As soon as he found it, he rubbed hard, his mouth on her clit at the same time, sucking and licking until she shook under him, calling out his name.

She came hard, her cunt soaking his hand and down his arm, and he didn't care. He just licked at her more until she shook again, coming right after the first. He loved how responsive she was, and couldn't wait to make her come again, this time around his cock. With a kiss to her pussy, he pulled away, licking his fingers while meeting her eyes.

"Owen." She tried to blink, but she was too far gone to even make out sensible words.

He quickly opened the condom and slid it down his length, needing to come harder than he ever thought possible. When he climbed up her body, placing kisses over her side and on her breast along the way, she tugged at his arms, bringing her closer.

"That was..." she trailed off, her eyes wide. "Holy God, Owen. I'm going to need you to do that again."

He grinned before stealing a kiss. "Whatever you say, babe. Whatever you say." Then he thrust into her in one move, and she screamed. She was so damn swollen that he knew he wouldn't last long, but he didn't care.

He'd already had the best pleasure ever by watching her come.

He pulled out slowly before thrusting back in. She wrapped one leg around his waist before bringing up the other to rest on his shoulder.

At his shocked look, she laughed. "Pilates."

"I've never wanted to cry in happiness during sex before, but dude. I think this is going to be amazing." He laughed before kissing her again.

Then he *moved.*

And she met him for every thrust, every roll of hips.

And when they both came, his heart raced, and his body grew sweat-slick. He shouted her name, taking her lips with his, knowing this had been far more than sex... far more than the best sex he'd ever had in his life.

This had meant something.

And from the panicked look in her eyes, she knew it, too.

Spent, he turned on his side, his cock still buried within her, and held her close, running his hands down her back. She didn't speak, but neither did he. He hadn't planned for this, hadn't planned on her.

And for someone like him, that couldn't end well.

He just hoped that somewhere, in all his past plans, he found a way to make this work.

Somehow.

Chapter Eight

Liz threw her head back and tried to catch her breath. It was pretty hard to do that with a dick in her mouth, and Owen's face firmly pressed between her legs. Her body was too sweat-slick to stay on top of him for long, so they'd shifted to their sides partially with her still somewhat covering him. She'd done a sixty-nine before, but with Owen, using her brain was always a little harder to do, and thinking was usually out the window as soon as their pants were off. Over the past two weeks of them finding every way they could to make each other come, she'd figured that out quickly.

"I can't keep this up if you're going to roll your tongue like that against my clit." She swallowed, the flavor of him on her tongue. It shouldn't turn her on as much as it did, but hell, she liked knowing he could taste her, as well.

He hummed, and she shut her eyes so she wouldn't come. "My cock is lonely, Liz. It needs your mouth."

She rolled her eyes, trying not to smile but totally doing it anyway. He was such a dork in bed, a sexy dork that could make her come with that mouth of his in like two seconds flat. Not to mention that it only took like three seconds with his cock. She was so easy when it came to Owen in bed, and yet her body didn't seem to care. The fact that she was made it so she wasn't easy at all when it came to everything outside of bed. She pushed at him daily, and he kept coming back for more. She knew she did it out of fear and a need to protect herself, but hell, he just continued to pursue her, and she kept allowing herself to be caught.

He did something particularly ingenious with his mouth right then, and she came, thoughts of worries and what the hell she was doing flying right out the window. He rolled them over and crawled over her before she could finish him off and then kissed her, their tastes mingling.

"I never seem to be able to give you a full blowjob," she complained, her legs wrapping around him of their own accord. "There was that one time, but it was only because you let me tie you to the bedposts." He'd tied her up the night before so he'd acquiesced to her teasing with silk scarves.

She almost came again just thinking about it.

He shrugged, his eyes brightening. "I get greedy and need this pussy." He reached between them and cupped her, making her eyes cross again. The man was a genius with his fingers, and it just wasn't fair. "I at least took out the piercings this time so you could have your way with me."

She petted him lazily up and down his back. He might be the most slender of his brothers, but his muscles were sleek, hard, and powerful. "I'm going to miss them inside me," she said honestly. She'd always been somewhat bold in bed, but Owen brought it out even more in her.

Owen kissed her softly. "Next time. You can do a whole study on the differences if you'd like."

Despite their positions, she giggled. "You're the one who likes doing things like that, Mr. Organization."

He nibbled up her jaw, his tongue darting out to soothe the spots he'd bitten. "You're a nurse, Lizzie. Science is your thing. Why don't we try a new position so we can see which one you like best? Then repeat it because repetition is key."

"You're a dork."

"But I'm your dork. And your dork is about to fuck you, so pick a position."

Your dork.

It had only been two weeks of them sleeping together, and already he was saying things like that. How could that be okay? How could she have let herself get into this position? With a shaky hand, she pushed at his shoulder so she rolled them over and she was on top. He let her move him easily, his hands resting on her hips as if they were meant to be there.

Maybe if she stayed on top, she could have a bit of control since she didn't seem to have any in any other parts of her life.

From the look Owen gave her, he understood what she was thinking all too well.

Just one more reason he scared her.

"You gonna move, or should I thrust up into you."

She shook her head, though the thought of him fucking *her* while she was on top had its merits. However, she needed to grab the reins so she knew she could leave if she wanted to. It was her only illusion of sanity. "I'll move."

Owen gripped her hips harder. "One sec." He reached over and fumbled around for the condom they'd laid out. They'd each been tested the previous week since oral sex still counted as sex and diseases could transfer, but they were still using condoms since Liz couldn't be on birth control. Her body was prone to blood clots and every single thing she'd tried in the past, including diaphragms, had led to complications and even hospitalization in one case.

So unless she wanted to get pregnant—something that wouldn't be happening *ever* if she had any say in the matter—she had to use condoms with each and every partner *every* time they had sex. She'd never had sex without a condom, so thankfully, she didn't know what she was missing—according to Tessa, anyway—but it was the principle of the matter. One day, her insurance would actually be able to cover tubal ligation for a single woman her age so she could protect her body and choices, but for now, condoms were it.

And she'd almost forgotten it just now.

Owen was seriously bad for her health.

"Put it on me?" Owen asked, his free hand sliding up her wrist. "You okay, babe? Need to stop?" The concern in his eyes speared into her, and she shook her head. This was just fun, sweaty sex. Nothing too personal. She didn't do personal. *Couldn't* do personal.

"Give it to me," she said, her voice a little snappish.

He rose a brow, that damn ring in it looking too sexy

for its own good. "I'm about to. But first I need to put the condom on."

She held out her hand. "I meant the condom, dork."

He grinned. "I love when you call me a dork because I'm pretty sure you're thinking of cruder words to call me but are trying to protect my little ol' feelings since my cock is resting next to your pussy. You're so sweet, Liz."

She rolled her eyes, a smile tugging at her lips as she grabbed the condom from him and tore it open. As she smoothed it down his length, wiggling back so she could cup his balls at the same time, Owen let out a groan.

"I fucking love your hands, babe. You can touch me any time you want."

She grinned. "Oh, yeah?" She reached over for the lube they'd used earlier when Owen had wanted to play with her ass a bit and squirted some on her hand. "What if I do this?"

She reached down to his cheeks and spread him a bit, using the lube on her fingers to press against his hole.

"Holy shit," he breathed. "Well, that wasn't what I had in mind, but if you want, I'm game."

She froze. "Seriously?"

He rose up on his forearms and gave her a serious look. "It's fair. You let me play with you with one finger earlier, so why not let you do the same for me? I hear that if you rub my prostate, it'll feel fucking amazing. And since we both just showered to prep you, I'm game."

She let out a breath. She'd only been slightly teasing, but now the idea of doing this seemed sexy as hell. "Okay, then, Owen. Lie back, turn your head, and cough."

He chuckled before letting out a long groan as she slowly breached him with her finger. She never thought this could be sexy, but with his hand on the base of his dick and the veins in his arm standing out from strain, she knew she'd never get this image out of her head.

She rubbed him slightly, finding the spot that sent his body into overdrive. "Here?" she asked.

"Holy hell. Yeah. There." He had his head back so she couldn't see his eyes, and for some reason, she wanted to. "God, I'm about to come just from that, but I'd rather come inside you." He panted the words, and she bit her lip, slowly working her way out of him.

When he reached and tugged on her arm, she let him pull her up so she hovered over him.

"Mouth, I need your mouth."

So she gave it to him. Their tongues tangled, their breaths syncing as she kissed him. His hands roamed over her, one resting on her butt, his fingers between her cheeks, the other sliding down to cup her breast.

"Ride me, cowgirl. Show me what you've got." He smacked her ass hard, and she let out a pained moan. Why did she like that? She sure as hell wasn't supposed to. "Come on, Liz. I want to see you."

She wiggled down slightly before reaching between them to guide him into her. Their eyes met as she slowly sank down, and her breath caught. When the backs of her eyes stung with unshed tears, she blinked them away, annoyed with herself for getting too close, for feeling too much.

This was just a fling.

It wasn't more.

It couldn't be more.

He gripped her hips, steadying her when she was fully seated. "You okay, Lizzie?" he rasped.

She nodded, lying to them both. "I need to move." That part wasn't a lie.

One hand slid up to cup her breast, his fingers playing with her nipple. "Then move, darling. Make yourself come on my cock."

She smiled then. "Oh, and what are you going to do, lazy butt?"

"Well, I would just lay here and think of England,

but I have a feeling your breasts are going to be too tantalizing to ignore."

She rolled her eyes before rolling her hips. When they both let out a gasp, she knew they were close. She didn't move off him; instead, she used his body to roll her hips over him, his length still fully inside her.

Their eyes locked once again, and though she tried to break the connection, she couldn't. His hands roamed over her, the caresses full of an emotion she couldn't name. And though she wanted to close her eyes and forget about what was happening, she didn't.

And when she came, her inner muscles tightening, he followed, his harsh shouts a balm to her soul even though they shouldn't be. Nothing was going as it should, damn it, and she was at a loss for what to do.

She collapsed on top of him, trying to catch her breath, aware if she spoke, she'd do the unmentionable thing and cry. She couldn't shed a tear, not for him, and surely not for herself.

Strong arms wrapped around her as Owen kissed the top of her head. "What's wrong, Lizzie. Talk to me."

Liz shook her head, curling more and more into herself even with him fully inside of her. She needed to get out of there, get out of the room, out of his arms, and into her clothes so she could once again find that steely control she'd worn like armor for as many years as she could remember.

Owen Gallagher was breaking her, and she couldn't let that happen.

When he slid his hand up and down her back, soothing her without words, she knew it was too much. She pulled away from him, letting him slide out of her, and she scrambled off the bed. She reached for her jeans, searching in vain for her underwear. They'd stripped each other in a hurry after dinner, and she wasn't sure she'd be able to find them in this panic of hers.

"Shit," Owen growled, reaching for the box of tissues on the nightstand. "Hold on a minute. What happened?" He cleaned himself off, disposing of the condom as he did so, and tried to reach for her.

She evaded his touch, her body shaking. "I need to go."

"It's your house, babe. Where do you need to go at ten at night?"

She slid on her jeans sans underwear. "I just need to go. God. Just let me be, Owen. The sex was great. Just get out, okay? I need...I need you to just go."

She stood in her darkened bedroom with only a small lamp to illuminate them both, wearing jeans and nothing else, her eyes stinging, and her breath coming in harsh pants. She knew she looked like a woman on the edge, but she didn't care. She just needed to breathe and not feel. If she felt...well, she knew what happened when she felt.

Owen had his hands up as if waving off a crazed bull. "Lizzie. Just sit down and tell me what happened. Did I hurt you? Was the anal play too much for you? Just tell me so I can fix it."

Her eyes narrowed. "You didn't hurt me." Not really. "You can't fix everything, Owen, even if that's what you seem to love to do."

He leaned back at the venom in her voice but didn't move away. "I don't know what I did to deserve that, but, yeah, I like fixing things. It's what I do."

"You can't fix me." To her horror, she felt a tear slide down her cheek, and she reached up to rub it away.

"I didn't say I wanted to," Owen said slowly as if talking her down from the ledge. Maybe she was already there and hadn't realized it. Either way, he needed to go so she could compose herself again. "Let's get you the rest of your clothes. Okay?"

"Why? Because you think I need a shield or something?" She did. "Just go. I can't think with you here, and you just can't be here right now. It was fun while it lasted, Owen. But I'm done. We both got off, so let's call this was it is. Over."

She knew she was being a bitch, but she couldn't help the words coming from her mouth. She hated herself more and more with each word she spoke, but she couldn't stop them once she'd begun. If she hurt him, if she made him leave, then maybe she wouldn't hurt him worse later. Maybe she wouldn't lie in pain, a thousand small cuts over her body as she wished for something that would never come.

Owen slid on his jeans and handed his shirt to her. "I can't find yours right now."

She took it greedily, awash in his scent as she tugged it on. That only made the tears fall faster. "Go."

He shook his head, coming closer to her. She had nowhere to back up, not with the bed in the way, so she couldn't stop him from gently putting his hands on her arms. "Honey. Liz. Talk to me. Why are you so scared? If I didn't hurt you during sex, then I must have done something for you to push me away like this. Yeah, I know you haven't wanted to open up with me at all since we started seeing each other, and I get that. We're still new, but you've never outright told me to get out before. What happened, Liz? You can talk to me. I promise. No matter what happens between us in bed or in our relationship, I want us to be friends."

She raised her chin. "We don't have a relationship."

The hurt in his eyes cut at her, and she wanted to crawl into a hole and hide. "Talk to me."

She huffed out a breath. "Fine. You want to know me? Want to know why I'm all fucked up and can't do anything right? Fine. Just take a seat and listen to the lonely and sad little life of Liz McKinley."

"Liz."

"I said sit." She closed her eyes tightly, willing back the tears. "Please."

The creak of the mattress made her open her eyes, and she let out a breath when she saw Owen sitting on the edge, his hand firmly clasped around hers. "Talk to me," he repeated.

"I don't do relationships."

"I figured that," Owen said slowly.

She shook her head. "I need to just get all of this out at once so don't interrupt."

He raised a brow but didn't comment again on her rudeness. Hell, she was well and truly a bitch, and he hadn't run yet. She didn't deserve him.

And she wouldn't have him.

"I don't do relationships because they don't work out. I watched my family fall apart, and it broke me. And when I finally thought I was happy and could have a relationship of my own once, everything got fucked up."

She tugged at his hand, and he let her go so she could pace. "My mom was—*is*—an alcoholic. She was a functional one, though, so no one really caught on that she was plastered most of the day rather than sober. She freaking drove me to school with a flask of vodka tucked in her purse, but no one cared. No one noticed that her smile was always a little too bright at PTA meetings and that she never actually fulfilled her promises about bake sales and crap like that because she was too drunk to do it."

She let out a breath, wrapping her arms around herself. Only the scent of Owen's shirt kept her settled, and that worried her. But soon he'd be gone. Soon, he'd know what kind of person she was, what kind of people she came from, and then she wouldn't have to worry about the way she wanted to be near him too much. She wouldn't have to worry that she'd end up turning into the monster her mother was...wouldn't have to worry she'd turn Owen into the shell her father had been.

She met Owen's gaze, but he kept to his word and didn't say anything. But she saw the fury in his eyes. The anger. Yet she couldn't see pity. She'd expected pity. She'd have been able to fight back pity. The fury? That she had no idea what to do with.

"She always yelled at me when we were home. Or when she wasn't yelling, it was that slurred calm voice that told me that bad things were coming. She hit me for the first time when I was six or seven. Slapped me right in the face because I needed a permission slip signed, and she hadn't been in the mood. She never stopped hitting me until I moved out. Every time I tried to fight back, she made it worse. And no one did a fucking thing."

When he finally spoke, it surprised her. "Where was your dad?"

She snorted; that same pain a hollow ache that never seemed to heal. She was a damn nurse, a healer, and yet she couldn't heal herself. She didn't want to. "Dear old Dad was there the whole time. He just didn't *care*. He watched her beat the shit out of me after calling me a whore and a lazy piece of crap, and he didn't do a single thing. He just didn't care anymore. She'd broken him long before she got to me. And yet he should have cared. He should have done something. But he didn't. He never fucking did. Then when I was fourteen, he just packed up everything and left. He fucking *left* me alone with her. Mom changed our names back to her maiden one the next year, but I still haven't heard from him. He could be dead for all I know, but hell, it's not like he'd have ever found a way to tell me if he's alive or not. So, yeah, relationships end up like that, Owen. At least with my blood, they do."

"Lizzie, that's on them. I could kill them for what they did to you, but that's on them."

"But they used to be happy. Then they had me and Mom started drinking. She hated the way she looked after the C-section. Hated the fucking scar and told me that often. Her boobs sagged after breastfeeding me, though she'd only done it a week before saying it hurt too badly. I went straight to formula after that, apparently. She told me she never had any time to do anything because she'd been strapped with a little blonde leech. And then, of course, Dad apparently didn't want her anymore after the baby, or so she said. So she would scream that she had to find men who actually wanted her since my dad was a useless piece of shit."

"Jesus Christ," Owen growled. "She told you all of that? How old were you?"

Liz shrugged, picking lint off his shirt. "Seven or so the first time, I think. I don't really remember since it's been most of my life. She was an abusive drunk who loved to throw words at Dad and me. Then when words weren't enough, she'd throw things at Dad since he didn't fight back. He'd been raised not to hit women, you see. But he never protected me. He just watched as she hit me with the belt, with her hand. I think the only time he stepped in was to tell her not to use the crystal glass she'd been drinking vodka out of on me. But that was probably because I'd end up in the hospital, or hell, because the crystal had been his mother's and given to them on their wedding day. I don't know."

Owen stood then, coming toward her, and she held out her hands, shaking her head. "Lizzie. None of that is on you. They should have gone to jail long before they ever had the chance to hit you a second time. Your dad too, Liz."

She pressed her lips together, her body oddly numb. "That's not the end of it, though. I can't *be* in a relationship, Owen. Things always get fucked up if I try."

He took another step forward. She took one back. "But we're not them. We're not any of them."

"But I'm my mother's daughter. My father's daughter. You see? When I was seventeen, I got to go to college since I worked my ass off to graduate early. I was smart, but not smart enough to get out of the city we grew up in. I found a boy who was nineteen, and I thought he liked me. Turned out he just liked my boobs or whatever. I found my mother *fucking* him in *my* dorm room two days after I gave the guy my virginity. I told the guy to get out, and my mom patted him on the cheek, telling him he was a good boy who needed to look higher for prime pussy. She was so drunk at that point, I don't think she could even put together sentences beyond that."

"That fucking little prick," Owen growled. He moved toward her so quickly, she didn't have a chance to back away. When he cupped her face, she didn't cry, she was all out of tears it seemed. "Lizzie, that's on pencil dick. Not you. None of this is your fault."

She blinked, unable to really hear him, not when she was in the past with her mother. Alone, so alone. So cold. "She beat the shit out of me that day, too. I don't even know why." Her voice sounded hollow to her ears, but maybe that was because she was so far away. "I dropped out of college the next day and moved the meager things I owned to another city and went to school there instead. The school wasn't as good, but without my mother's lack of income to get me grants and financial aid, I couldn't really afford anything better. But I met Tessa, so I guess everything worked out in the end."

His thumb traced her cheek. "And you haven't been with anyone since then?"

"Not in a relationship. I've had sex because that's all there is for me, Owen. That's all there can be. My mother used to be a nice, sweet girl before she met my father. My dad had apparently been a gentleman before my mother went off the rails. They broke each other, and I refuse to do that to anyone." She stepped back. "I refuse to do that to you."

He shook his head, his eyes sad—yet they held no pity for her. "Lizzie, that's not how things work. We aren't our parents."

"Your parents were amazing, though. So you can't really say anything."

"My parents worked themselves to the bone for us and neglected themselves. I don't want to be my parents."

"Don't compare them," she said softly. She'd tried to snap at him, but she found herself unable to find the energy. "Just go. Please. I just need you to go."

In the distance, she heard the front door open and knew Tessa had come home from work. Liz could talk to Tessa if she needed to, but right then, she just wanted to be alone.

Owen studied her face before slowly lowering his hands. "I'm going." Her heart splintered. "But I'm not going for good. I'm not leaving you, Liz. I'm letting you breathe. But I'm coming back, damn it. I'm coming back." With that, he placed a gentle kiss on her forehead before leaving her in her bedroom and walking out in only his jeans.

She heard him murmur to Tessa, but Liz couldn't hear the words. She just slowly slid to her knees, her eyes unseeing, her senses dulled. Dimly, she heard Tessa move into the room, barely felt the other woman's hands on her shoulders.

But when her best friend held her close, Liz finally did the one thing she'd promised herself she would never do.

She wept.

Chapter Nine

"Call it. Time of death, five forty-two p.m."

Liz stood motionless as Dr. Wilder's words hit her, the meaning of them crashing into her far harder than they should. She didn't know this patient, had only been working on the man for seven minutes since she'd been called into the room late as additional support, and yet the words broke her ever so slightly.

She'd known her job would entail this when she signed up for nursing school. There had been no hiding from the dark parts of the job, even as a student. Yet she'd also known that saving people's lives would be worth it. It had to. She'd saved countless lives, helped others through the ER when she thought she wouldn't be able to, and yet today, she hadn't been enough. The doctors, techs, nurses, and aides hadn't been enough for this man and the car accident that had been too much for his body.

This had been the second patient today that had died when she was in the room. Twice, time of death had been called. Twice, they hadn't been enough. Twice, others had had to come into the room and clean up the mess left behind, the only evidence that someone had once been alive in the room but would now forever be lost to the powers that were far stronger than the strength in the hands of the doctors, nurses, and staff who'd tried to save them. It wasn't uncommon to lose more than one person in a day, not in a trauma center, but today of all days seemed harder. Did it ever get easier?

Damn it.

Damn it all.

Fuck it all.

Just fuck everything.

After almost an hour of crying the night before, she'd finally fallen asleep in Tessa's arms, her body drained. Thankfully, she had a swing shift today, so she'd been able to sleep in a bit, her body heavy from sobbing and too many emotions warring within her mind and soul. She hadn't meant to tell Owen everything or, honestly, anything at all. Pushing him away had been the only way to keep things safe, and yet, in the end, she wasn't sure how much good it had done. He'd said he would be back, but would he? He now knew the darkest parts of her, the parts she'd wanted to keep hidden but had let bleed out in a rush.

Damn it. It didn't matter. She was at work, and she couldn't think about Owen or anything having to do with him. She needed to clean herself up and try to keep the next patient alive. Because if she lost this one... She held back a shudder. She couldn't think like that. It wouldn't do anyone any good.

"Liz? Can I speak to you for a minute?"

Liz jolted at Nancy's question and gave a quick nod. "Sure. Where?"

"The lounge, please," she clipped before moving quickly away with Lisa on her tail.

After letting out a sigh, Liz followed them, the knot in her stomach tightening with each step. Nancy didn't have the ability to fire her, but she would be the one to let everyone know who would be let go with the upcoming budget cuts. Liz just prayed today wasn't the day because she really wasn't sure she'd make it through it.

Liz got waylaid by two doctors asking questions on her way to the lounge, so she was almost ten minutes late by the time she made it in there. And while she might have been doing her job, from the look on Nancy's face, being late was a cardinal sin.

"Sorry I'm late, Dr. Mendez and Dr. Johnson needed a few questions answered." She went straight to the coffee pot and poured herself some, seeing as Nancy and Lisa had already done the same for themselves.

"Hmm," Nancy said dismissively.

God, sometimes Liz truly hated her job, and today was just one of those days that amplified that fact. Usually, she just had to think of the patients she could help in order to keep going, but it was a little harder today, and she resented that.

If only she'd kept her mouth shut to Owen and walked away when she'd had the chance to keep her head held high. If she had, she wouldn't have started down this path of self-pity and doubt.

Once again, she pushed thoughts of Owen from her mind and focused on what was in front of her. Namely, *who* was in front of her.

"Take a seat, Liz," Nancy said after a moment. "We don't have a lot of time to talk now thanks to the delay."

Liz held back a retort as the "delay" had been work-related, and the three of them were on the clock and had *countless* things to do. She took a seat across from the two of them, feeling as if she were headed into her own inquisition.

"Yes?"

"As you know, the budget is set to be finished by the end of next week. Repercussions for that decision will trickle down, but as we all know, cutbacks are usually swift and without mercy in our department."

Liz's hands cupped her mug tightly. "So the cutbacks in our department are true, then?" Though, officially, there had only been rumors for the past couple of months, they'd had enough ring of truth to them that everyone took them as fact.

Nancy nodded, giving Lisa a look Liz couldn't interpret. "Yes, we will be losing at least one nursing position, and perhaps a second if things shift the way they look to be."

Two positions? Holy hell. Liz had no idea how the ER was supposed to get by losing one nurse, let alone two.

"Do they realize upstairs that we're already working long hours and don't have enough staff?" Liz asked, her mind whirling.

Nancy shrugged. "We're just the underlings, Liz. Get used to it. But I called you both in here because you're the two senior nurses under me. I cannot guarantee either of your jobs as that's not my place, but performance reviews will most likely be part of the decision. Losing one or both of you will hurt, but it would

169

help the budget according to my sources. We just don't have the funding." She met Liz's gaze, but Liz didn't blink.

Her performance reviews were stellar, far better than Lisa's, and everyone in this room knew it. But the rumors about Owen and Murphy hadn't quit thanks to Lisa constantly churning up the waters.

Liz would not let this petty bullshit cost her her job, however. She slid her chair back, the scraping sound echoing in the almost empty room. "Okay, then. When you have real details, let me know. I need to get back to work as the place can't run itself."

Lisa rolled her eyes but didn't say anything. Liz was about two eye rolls away from slapping the other woman so she turned away and started walking. She was *not* a violent person. Each time she even thought about doing something like that, she became more like her mother, and she'd be damned if she let that happen. That was why punching Owen like she had before had made her act as she had. That was *not* Liz—no matter what vile things her mother had put into her head. If only she could keep remembering that.

Another hour passed during her shift, and the tension pulsating in her temples had yet to abate. She only had another hour or so go to before she could go home, but her feet were pretty much done. With a sigh, she glared at her orthopedics. It looked like it was time to get a new pair and break them in because if her feet hurt like this already, the darn shoes were on their way out.

She kept her focus on her patients—the only people that mattered today—and ignored the whispers surrounding her. Apparently, Lisa was doing her best to keep the "Get Liz Fired" campaign going strong.

Liz hadn't done a single fucking thing wrong, however, and she had to keep remembering that. Lisa was just scared about her job and going about keeping it in an immature and shitty way. It wasn't Liz's fault that Lisa was so insecure she was spreading rumors about Liz and her patients. But hell, the fact that Liz *knew* people she'd thought of as friends were talking about her killed her.

"Yeah, I don't know which patient she's with, but it might be both, you know?" another nurse, Freddie, said. "The way I hear it, she's not really picky when it comes to getting it on after work. I mean, if she has all this time to make it with the people she treats, maybe she shouldn't be here."

"Yeah, we're a good hospital. We don't need that kind of negativity or reputation."

Liz froze in her tracks on her way to the next patient, her blood boiling even as her stomach dropped.

Dear God. Was that what people really thought of her? That she was some slut who jumped from bed to bed and didn't care about work?

Well, for fuck's sake, if she wanted to sleep with twenty guys in twenty days on her own time, she could if she wanted to. She was a single woman, who didn't need to be ashamed about whom she slept with. Owen and Murphy weren't her patients anymore, and she'd already told herself she wouldn't treat them if for some reason fate led them through the door once again. These people were just petty fucking idiots that made her want to scream.

And there was nothing she could do about it.

She closed her eyes and took a deep breath; actually, there *was* something she could do about it. This wasn't high school, and she wasn't the lonely teenager too scared and shy to say anything.

She pulled back the curtain where the two nurses were cleaning up something and raised a brow. "You might want to make sure that the person you're gossiping about isn't right behind you."

The younger nurse, Lydia, had the grace to blush. Freddie, one of Lisa's friends, just rolled her eyes. Seriously, did these women have no self-respect or *any* other way to react?

"First, we're at work. Get your mind on your patients, and off whatever gossip you hear about me. Second, if I wanted to date someone out of this hospital, it has no bearing on my performance. Third, if I wanted to date the whole damn Denver Broncos starting line-up, provided they were single, it wouldn't be any of your business. So maybe you should stop finding ways to cut another woman down and get to work. Because if you're spending so much time worrying about who I might be sleeping with, you're ignoring those who actually need your help."

With a huff, Liz stomped away and toward her next patient, aware that the staff was staring at her. Thankfully, the ER wasn't that full today, and she'd been in the corner where they hadn't yet admitted the next set of patients. With her voice as low as she'd made it, no one would have heard her other than the janitor and a few other coworkers.

Hell, she'd made a fool of herself, but she was beyond caring. She just needed to keep people safe, stop the bleeding, keep their bodies intact, and walk away from whatever mess she might have just made.

She was just so tired of it all.

So an hour later, after she'd cleared her patients, made sure the next nurse would know what to do, and had grabbed her things, she shouldn't have been surprised that her day wouldn't actually end the way she wanted.

Owen stood near the front doors, two paper cups of coffee in his hands as he leaned against the wall. He wore a very sexy leather jacket over his usual attire of slacks and a nice shirt, and she really wanted to gobble him up.

But this was her place of business.

The same place that made her feel like *nothing*.

The place that made her feel as if everything she did was wrong—including knowing Owen and Murphy.

And the last time she'd seen Owen, she'd broken in front of him after laying everything on the table.

This was so not her day.

"Tessa said you were off shift," he said as he handed her a cup—the one with the L on the side.

She wasn't going to smile and let that warm feeling spread through her at the sight of his cute organization.

Liz ignored the looks from the other nurses and orderlies in the room. "Oh? She's working the late shift tonight so she must be on her way in."

Owen nodded. "She knocked on my door when I got home from work since her battery apparently died in her car."

"Hell. I keep telling her she needs to replace that old thing."

"And she probably would if she hadn't just bought a house," he replied. "Which she explained in detail after calling the car all sorts of names not fit for public. But I offered to drop her off here. She said she has a key to your car, and mentioned that she could take yours home after her shift so I can take you home now."

Liz raised a brow. How nice was it that everyone was planning her life for her. Nancy, Lisa, Tessa, and now Owen.

"She texted all of this to you, aware you only answer work things during your shift."

"I could have taken the bus," she replied.

"But you don't have to. So say, 'thank you, Owen,' and come with me." He leaned forward so only she could hear him. God knew what others thought just then, but she truly didn't care anymore. She'd said her piece. "I know I'm one of the last people you want to see right now, but I told you I wasn't going away anytime soon. So, come on, Liz. Let me take you home."

She let out a breath. "Okay." He gave her a pointed look. "Thank you for the ride."

Owen smiled widely, and she was pretty sure Lisa and Freddie gasped softly behind her. Yeah, Owen in a leather jacket was sexy. Owen smiling while wearing a leather jacket was something else altogether.

And, apparently, he'd claimed her as his.

Now Liz just had to figure out how what she was going to do about it.

* * *

Owen was exhausted and yet exhilarated at the same time. Now that he was alone in his small hotel room with the TV on low, talking about the news of the day, he could undo his tie and try to relax a bit before things got interesting. He'd spent the entire day in meetings with the Roland Group, going over the final details of the upcoming project. He had a great feeling about it. They'd seemed truly excited about the proposal Owen had laid out. He didn't have the final plans, as he'd need Murphy and Graham for that, but he had enough that he knew no one could walk away from this unless they were holding onto loyalties that didn't make sense. He might not be in his own bed that night and was missing Liz something fierce, but as soon as he got home, he'd celebrate.

Well, as soon as Clive Roland signed on the dotted line, that was.

Gallagher Brothers Restoration worked on a varied amount of projects throughout the year. Sometimes, they worked on homes; other times, on large estates or businesses, doing their best to keep the history alive and honored while at the same time upgrading and modern-izing some things for safety and convenience. It was a delicate balance, but it was what they excelled at. Between the four Gallaghers, they each got the job done, and had slowly but surely been gaining a reputation for good, solid work, as well as meeting their deadlines.

It was everything they had wanted in the first and second phases of their company projection plan. Okay, maybe it was *Owen's* plan, but the others had been on board since he'd made them color-coded charts and graphs. Owen was the one who planned and set things up, Murphy made sure their ideas would actually work as well as stay in line with their goals, and Graham made sure things got done. And, in the end, Jake came in to make sure the other three knew what they were doing and could mesh it all together.

They always worked as a team on each part, which made the fact that Owen was here on his own a bit different. But the others had been so busy with their other projects that they'd pushed Owen into taking over the initial business proposals and getting things signed. They would come in later and finish the mock-ups as well as do the heavy lifting once everything had been signed. He'd shown his plans to the others, of course, and they'd agreed on everything, but this was truly on

Owen's shoulders this time. It wasn't how they normally worked, but Owen hadn't really minded. He liked the responsibility and knowing that he was actually producing something that could be worked with. Each of them knew how to do each other's jobs in case they needed to switch off, but they also had their specialties.

It was nice getting his hands deep into the project from the start and knowing that he would be part of something that was his idea and that his brothers actually agreed with him. It wasn't always easy to work with family—especially his family since they were all loud, bearded, and tended to punch first and ask questions later—but they got shit done.

And after today's meetings, Owen would get even *more* shit done.

This project, in particular, was special because of the land it was on. It wasn't just one house or one estate; it was an entire central town that needed to be restored. An entire Main Street in a small, Artisan, mountainside town outside of Denver that wanted to attract more tourists in the ever-competing market. Owen's plans were to use what they had and *enhance* the history of the place while cleaning it up. He knew some would start from scratch and make it look as if it were a newly faced historical landmark. Meaning they'd bulldoze their way through it and build new while trying to make it look like it had been there the whole time. That was the faster way to get things done, but Owen didn't like it. It wouldn't stay true to the bones of the buildings, and the area's rich history.

The Roland Group had seemed to agree with him, and now he only had to wait for Clive to call and let him know what direction the Group was going.

Of course, that meant Owen was alone in a hotel room, away from his family and the woman he wanted to spend time with. He'd call Liz his girlfriend, but that word would scare her so he would be a little more careful. At least, she hadn't pushed him away recently. In fact, they'd almost been acting like a tried and true couple, going out on dates and spending time together rather than hiding what they had and what they were to each other in the bedroom.

Maybe he *should* call her his girlfriend just to see what she did.

And maybe he should stop thinking like he was in high school and get over himself.

His phone buzzed on the nightstand, and he scrambled to pick it up, only to deflate when he saw Murphy's name.

"What's up?" he answered.

"I'm just working late on the Jefferson project and

was getting a little slap happy. I thought I'd call and see how things went."

Owen sat up a little straighter, trying to get comfortable. Hotel beds were never as good as his own, in his opinion. Plus, he always did his best not to think about what kind of germs lived on the damn thing.

He held back a shudder before speaking. "How are the plans coming? I know you wanted to do that addition on the back, but the couple wasn't sure about how big they wanted it to be."

Murphy mumbled something Owen couldn't catch, and he smiled. Murphy might look like the baby-faced Gallagher, but he cursed more than any of them. "These damn people keep changing their minds, hence why I'm working late. I finally figured I'd just draw up five different plans and see which one they like."

"And if they choose none of them?"

"They'll fucking choose one. Even if I have to have you add colored-coded charts onto it to explain how amazing my work is."

Owen snorted. "I can add color-coded charts to anything you want. Just ask."

Murphy sighed. "I just might. This couple spends more time fighting with each other than me, at least, but I don't know how well it's all going to work out."

Owen ran a hand through his hair, noting he needed

a haircut soon. "They fight but then they look at each other after they do and you know they're just growling at each other so they can make out later. Graham and Blake do the same thing."

"And Maya, Jake, and Border," Murphy added with a laugh. "Hell, you and Liz fight just the same way."

Owen couldn't help but smile. "And the making up part is worth it." Usually, but he wasn't going to get into that. He and Liz were slowly working on what they had, and he'd just bide his time until they could take things to the next level.

"Whatever you say, man. Anyway, you never answered my question. How's the deal going?"

"Good, so far. They really liked what I had to say about our plans. Since it's a board and not just one person, they have to make a decision as a group, so it's taking a while." Longer than he'd hoped, but this was the first time they'd worked with such a large group outside of their normal area of the city.

"Makes sense. Hey, Owen? I don't know if we said it earlier, but Graham and I really appreciate you doing all of this. I know the three of us usually do this part together, but these past couple of months have been crazy. We won't force you into this position again, though because I know you've been doing twice the amount of work you normally do, and that's not exactly fair."

Owen frowned. "We're a unit, Murphy. If someone needs to pick up the slack, we do it. And you know I don't mind organizing things."

His baby brother laughed. "I know you don't. I swear you were reorganizing my stuffed animals by size before I could walk."

"Well, of course. They needed to be properly aligned so you could have maximum playing time."

"You're an idiot, but we love you. Okay, I need to get back to this project from hell. Text the rest of us when you hear any news."

"Will do."

They ended the call, and Owen rested his head against the headboard. He wanted to go to bed, but he had a couple of hours yet where Clive could call. He let out a breath, staring at his phone. Maybe he'd call Liz and see how she felt about phone sex before he went to bed. That was something they hadn't tried as of yet.

As soon as he reached for his phone, however, it lit up with Clive Roland's name on the screen. Heart racing, he picked up, doing his best to keep his voice casual.

"Hey, Clive. Good to hear from you."

"Owen. Good, good. Well, I'm sorry to say this over

the phone since that's not how I like to do things, but you're a young kid, so you understand. The board has decided to go in another direction that will be more cost effective for us. We know this other firm better, and since they have connections to our board, we feel like it would be the best idea. Thank you for showing us what you have, but as you know, kid, business is business, and you can't win them all."

Clive ended the call before Owen could even say a fucking word.

Was this really happening? Had Owen actually lost out on the job that would put the Gallaghers through to the next year? Holy hell. He'd lost it all. He'd fucking *lost*. To a company that had lower standards, cheaper products, and *connections* to the board.

His palms went clammy, and he tried to catch his breath but found he couldn't. Sweat trickled down his back, and he forced himself to move so his feet were off the bed, pressing to the floor as if he were trying to ground himself.

He'd failed.

How was he supposed to tell his brothers that all his hard work, all the time he'd put in alone and without them had been for nothing? They'd have to find other projects to fit into the timeframe they'd laid out for this large one, and he wasn't sure if they would be able to do it. It had been a calculated risk, but they'd all agreed to it.

They'd all agreed to it because they trusted Owen.

And he'd failed.

His phone buzzed again, and he swallowed hard before looking at the readout. Hands shaking, he answered. "Liz."

"What's wrong?" she asked, her voice soft. "I was calling to see how you were after your long day, but you sound like someone stole your puppy. Talk to me, baby."

She never called him baby. How bad did he sound?

"I lost the job." Not we. Not the company. *He* did. And, somehow, he had to figure out a way to make it better, but he didn't know how.

"What the fuck is that client thinking? I'm so sorry, Owen." He'd told her before about the project, but hadn't mentioned names or too many details since those were under lock and key. Now, it didn't seem important.

"I'm sorry, too."

"Damn it. Do you want to drive home now? Or want me to come up there?"

He shook his head, though she couldn't see him. "It's two hours at least, and it's dark out. I'll just be back tomorrow." The fact that she'd offered warmed him a little, though he wasn't sure if he'd ever truly thaw from this.

"That fucker. Okay, get into something comfortable and then get in bed. Maybe phone sex will make this night better."

Owen barked out a laugh and gripped his phone harder. "Thank you, Liz. Just...just thank you."

"Anything, Owen. You know that. Anything."

And he did know, though he still knew things were on shaky ground between them. Hell, everything he had was tentative these days. But the sound of her voice, the sound of her laugh...that helped.

He just didn't know if it was enough.

If anything was enough.

Chapter Ten

Once again, Liz's feet hurt, and she wanted to just soak in her old tub and forget about the long day. Only she couldn't, since she'd made plans with Owen and she was pretty sure her tub had a small leak anyway. It was just one more thing on her household list that never seemed to end, and she had a feeling that soon she'd have to ask the Gallaghers for help.

She hated asking for help.

Liz let out a snort as she toed off her work shoes. Yeah, the fact that she hated asking for help wasn't a surprise at all. She'd rather throw herself on an anthill most days than show someone she couldn't do things on her own. That's probably why she was currently exhausted, hating her job, and in need of a bubble bath she couldn't have.

Maybe drinking tonight with Owen would help.

Or sex. Yes, sex would help tremendously.

How she'd gone from avoiding him to needing him in her life she didn't know, and she didn't want to think about it. If she kept dwelling on it, she'd end up fucking things up again. He hadn't run away when she'd bared her past to him; instead, he pushed at her harder to let go. So maybe if they were careful, if they took things slowly, they might have a shot.

She had one leg out of her pants and froze, her gaze meeting her reflection in the mirror.

A shot? She was at the point where she was thinking about having *a shot* with Owen? And not the alcoholic kind. The kind that meant futures and having trust in someone, believing that they wouldn't screw everything up where they left you bleeding and broken on the ground.

How had this happened?

And more importantly, did she *want* this to happen?

Liz blinked at her reflection before letting out a breath. It was just one more date, one more day with a man that confused her to no end. This wasn't a proposal for something more. She just had to take it one day at a time and not stress herself out as much as she was.

Between work, her house, and Owen, she was going to end up with an ulcer.

Okay, time to get over herself, and get her mind in the game. She had a date with a very sexy man tonight, and if everything worked out, she'd have a few orgasms, as well. Owen was good with his hands in and out of bed. She blushed. Okay, fine, so she was one lucky woman. She just had to remember that. And as long as she didn't think about how she could mess things up, she'd be fine.

She jumped in the shower quickly, washing away the day and the stress of the job, knowing she didn't have much time to get ready before Owen showed up. Thankfully, she'd chopped off a few inches of her hair the week before so it wouldn't take her hours to blow dry it like usual. Thirty minutes later, she had her hair as done as it was going to get, a little bit of makeup on, and a wrap dress Tessa had made her buy over a year ago that she hadn't had a chance to actually wear yet.

She'd put on patterned tights, and was just about to get into her knee-high boots when the doorbell rang. As Tessa was already out on her date for the evening—a second date with a man from an online dating site—Liz scrambled to the door, boots in hand.

On the other side, Owen stood on her small porch, the dark coal of his trousers looking sexy as hell on those thick, muscled legs of his. He had on a long-sleeved dress shirt that was a few shades lighter than his pants, and hadn't bothered with a tie or overcoat. Instead, he wore the leather jacket that she loved and made her want to dry hump him right there on the porch.

From the knowing look in his eyes, he had the same idea.

"I'm almost ready."

Owen's gaze traveled over her body, and he licked his lips. "We could just stay here, you know. I'll help you into those boots, and then I'll strip down those tights of yours so I can fuck you from behind. Of course, I'd have to lick up that pretty ass of yours because damn, honey, that dress just makes your curves stand out so everyone knows they're perfect for my hands."

She rolled her eyes, even as her body heated at his words. "It's a wrap dress, so it's supposed to make my curves all sexy-like. According to Tessa anyway."

Owen stepped forward so he could close the door behind him before reaching out and tracing his finger over the side of her breast. "Tessa's right. And a wrap dress? Does that mean I get to unwrap you later?"

Liz leaned forward and kissed his stubbled jaw. "That's the general idea. But seriously, I'm hungry, and you promised me a date. We can have all the sex you want when we get back, but I skipped lunch thanks to an emergency, and I'm starving."

Owen frowned before going over to pick up her coat off the rack by the door. "Let's get you fed then, Lizzie. But you know that you shouldn't skip meals. You're a nurse."

Liz finished zipping up her boots and turned her back so Owen could help her into her jacket. "Yeah, well, nurses and doctors have horrible diets. We eat what's on hand, and rely on coffee to get through the day. While I'd love to be able to say I eat salads at lunch and hydrate, I totally don't." She turned and Owen pressed a small kiss to her lips. Her damn traitorous heart sped at the touch, and she did her best not to lean into him and demand more.

"Let's feed you, then. And hydrate. Then I'll work out the kinks in your back by fucking you until we're both exhausted."

She grinned at him as he opened the door for her. "That sounds like a plan, Gallagher. Food and sex. What more could a girl ask for?"

Owen gave her an odd look she couldn't decipher before blanking his face. She'd said something that either irritated him or made him think, and she had a feeling it had to do with the fact that she kept pushing him away, ever so subtly. Damn it, she needed to do better, but it was reflex, after all.

The drive to the restaurant Owen had made reservations for wasn't uncomfortable, and for that she was grateful. He asked about her day, and she told him all she could without going into details. Not only did she not want to break patient confidentiality, she knew ER room visits weren't the best thing to talk about over dinner.

The place Owen had chosen for dinner was near the main downtown area of Denver, but not in the busy part where it was hard to find parking. Apparently, Owen's sisters-in-law worked at a tattoo shop near there with Maya actually owning half of it. Maybe if Liz ever had a moment to herself, she'd stop by and see if she could get something small. She loved the look of Owen's ink, and she'd always wanted something for herself.

When she'd told Owen that over appetizers, his eyes had darkened. "What would you get?"

Liz smiled. "You like the idea, then?"

Owen reached over their plates to trace the back of her hand with his finger, and she shivered. "Yeah, I do. I think your body was made for art."

He'd whispered the words, but she still blushed at the idea that others could hear. While she liked to talk dirty and in detail, she preferred to do it behind closed doors. Owen didn't seem to have that problem.

"Um...I was thinking of maybe something to do with healing, like a symbol, color, or flower that represents healing and rebirth. Probably on my hip or lower back since those parts are always hidden under my scrubs. I'll have to do more research."

Owen nodded before moving his hand back and taking a sip of his wine. They'd both ordered a glass of shiraz to go with their meals and would stop at one drink since they had to drive home later.

"Maya or Blake could do that for you. Hell, anyone at Montgomery Ink would make it work. Everyone at the shop has their specialties, but I think Callie, one of the other women who works there, is a flower whiz. She's newer than the others, but from what I've seen, she knows what she's doing."

Liz took a bite of her meal before continuing, "Are all of your tattoos from that shop, then?"

Owen nodded. "I was late to the game with my ink because I spent so long researching exactly what I wanted. Then Jake met Maya in a bar, and they became best friends. Once I saw what she—as well as her brother and the rest of them—could do, I knew who would be doing my ink." He snorted. "And it's not like I could go anywhere else after that, or Maya would have kicked my ass."

Liz smiled widely. "I think I love Maya and Blake because of that. They don't take shit from anyone."

Owen quirked a brow, the ring there small enough that most people missed it, but still there to show that he wasn't always the man in the suit. "You don't take it from anyone either, Liz."

She shrugged, moving out of the way as the waiter took away their appetizer plates and set down their entrees.

"Did I say something wrong?" Owen asked.

She looked up at him and shook her head. "No, you didn't. I just don't really think I compare to either of them. They're so strong."

"And so are you. I know you don't see yourself that way, but I can tell you that neither of them did either. About themselves. Hell, I'm pretty sure we all have days where we don't feel like we can handle things. It's how we work through those times and persevere that defines our strength."

She tilted her head as she studied his face. "You're much wiser than you let on, Gallagher."

He grinned. "Yeah? I don't always feel wise." His grin fell, and she wanted to reach out and hold him. The table and food between them stopped her, but only just.

"It's been a week since you got back," she treaded carefully. "Is everything okay with you and your brothers?"

Owen looked down, playing with his food. It was so unlike him that she knew he was really worried. "I guess. I mean they keep saying they don't blame me for what happened but I don't know. Deals fall through all the time, but this one...this one hurt."

She reached out and gripped his free hand. "Listen to your brothers, Owen. They're telling you that they don't blame you, and you know what, I bet they don't. You all work so hard on a company you built with your own hands, and I am so proud of you guys. So you don't have that one client, that's fine. You'll have twenty more. You guys have a wonderful reputation, and you're going to make it. I've seen the work you guys do."

"This one just hurts, you know?"

"I know," she whispered. This one had been on him, and he was taking it personally. She couldn't blame him for his feelings as she'd have been in the same boat, but it still hurt her to see him like this. "How about I let you work on a few things in my house? Would that make you feel better?" She didn't know anything else she could do for him, and honestly, she needed to get over herself and ask for help in things she couldn't do on her own. Tessa had already been on her for that and had wanted to ask the Gallaghers weeks ago.

Maybe it was time for Liz to listen.

He squeezed her hand, his eyes lightening. "You must feel sorry for me if you're asking for help."

"I'd flip you off, but we're in a nice restaurant and I'm hungry."

"You can fuck me later to make your point known," Owen whispered.

Her heart sped up again, and her breath quickened. "Good."

Owen had her on her knees in his bathroom as he thrust his hips into hers, their bodies in sync as they panted together. They might have both been clothed, but she knew she was close to coming from the friction alone. They'd finished their meals rather quickly at the restaurant, talking about things that mattered but weren't going to lead them down roads better left untraveled, before paying with cash and practically running out of the building.

Anyone who looked at them would have known what they were racing off to do, but she hadn't cared. The ride had been achingly long, and she'd literally had to sit on her hands so she wouldn't reach over and undo

Owen's pants. There was no way she'd get them both into an accident because she couldn't keep herself from touching him.

As soon as they'd pulled into his driveway since it would have been silly for him to park in hers as they were neighbors, they'd thrown themselves at each other, kissing, pulling, and kneading. Somehow, they'd made their way into his house, not making a decision on which bed to sleep in as it didn't matter. She just needed *him*.

When he'd pressed her against the front door, she'd winced, her body sore from a long day's work. Owen had taken one look at her and decreed that they'd be taking a bath to soak before they fucked like rabbits.

She loved that mouth of his.

And that mouth was currently sliding down her back over the material as he reached forward to undo her dress. She pulled away and twisted so she was kneeling in front of him still, but this time, facing him.

"We can't even make it far enough to stand and strip," she said, her breathing heavy.

"I need my hands on you," Owen said with a groan. "What can I say? Now, there was a mention earlier of unwrapping. Can I play now?"

She smiled widely, loving the way he pouted. God, she could fall for this man. And that's why she would do her best not to think about it, or she'd scare herself out of his arms and out of this relationship.

"Just pull the tie at the side. Then the other underneath on the other. Then you'll see your present."

Owen gave her a hard kiss before leaning back. "It's like Christmas morning."

"Uh huh. Now strip me because you promised me a bath to soak before you fucked me, and with the way we're going, we'll end up skipping the bath and my feet will hate you for that."

"I don't want your feet hating me." He leaned forward and undid the ties, his eyes on her body as her dress fell to the sides. She rolled her shoulders, and the rest of the fabric pooled by their knees. Owen's eyes darkened, his gaze traveling over the black lace bra and panty set she'd worn under the knit dress. "You're wearing garters," he breathed, his voice cracking slightly. "And the belt thing that keeps your stockings up." He met her gaze, his eyes narrowing. "You said you were wearing tights. Not stockings. How could you keep something this fucking sexy from me?"

She grinned before cupping her breasts. "What?" She blinked innocently. "I told you that you would be unwrapping your present."

He growled before crushing his mouth to hers, one hand thrust into her hair, the other on her ass, molding, his fingers playing with her crack. "I'm going to fuck this ass tonight, Liz. You're ready for me, for my cock. So we're going to soak and get our bodies all limber and hot, then I'm going to fuck your ass and have you squeeze my dick as you come. Does that sound like a plan?"

Liz gave him a bland look. "It's all lollipops and rainbows before someone mentions butt sex."

Owen blinked before he threw back his head and laughed. "Yes, butt sex changes everything. So, what do you say?"

He gave one cheek a squeeze, and her body shivered. She clung to him, needing, aching, *ready*. "Is that punishment for keeping my garters from you?"

He pulled her hair slightly so her head fell back and he could meet her eyes. "Not a punishment, Lizzie. A promise." He let out a shuddering breath. "And because I really want us in the tub to get clean for later, I'm going to have to watch you take off your stockings and bra. I don't think I'm going to be able to do it for you, or I'll end up bending you over the edge of the tub and having my way with you. We're going slow." He let out a deep breath. "Well, as slow as we can."

She laughed, shaking her head. "Knowing us, that's not really slow."

He winked at her as he leaned back so he could stand up. When he reached for her, she placed her hand in his and stood up on shaky legs. She wore only her boots and underthings, and knew the image would be burned into his brain forever. It damn well should have because the look he gave her now would forever be burned into hers.

Knowing if she teased them, they'd end up missing out on the bath she so desperately wanted, she quickly stripped as he did the same. They'd play with her outfit again another time when they both weren't already so close to the edge that they were ready to fall.

Owen got in first, the water up to his chest. The tub was large enough for three people at least, and Liz knew it was custom-made. Perhaps dating someone who owned a construction company was a good idea, after all. He held her hand as she got in, the water so hot that it almost scalded, but it was just how she liked it.

She sank into the tub, her back to his front, and sighed. His cock was hard and pressed firmly between her cheeks, but she didn't care. She was the most comfortable she'd been in months.

"This is paradise."

Owen kissed behind her ear. "Just wait." He reached around and pressed a button and she gasped. He'd turned on the jets, the bubbles around them sizzling on her skin.

"Oh, yeah, I could totally live in here."

He licked up her ear, nibbling on the lobe. "Anytime you want, babe. The tub is yours."

"I think I only want you for your tub." She had her eyes closed, and though she was teasing, she still jumped when he cupped her below the water. "Owen."

"Only the tub, huh? I'll have to be sure to change that. I'm going to wash you to get you ready for after our bath. Just sit here and relax, Liz. You don't have to do anything except *be*."

She kept her eyes closed, knowing she could get used to this far too easily. Owen used his hands, not a loofa or washcloth, to clean her body. He had peach-scented soap she'd never seen him use before, and knew he'd bought it for her. She had her head leaned back, resting on one of his shoulders as his hands caressed her arms, her shoulders, her neck. Then he went down below to clean her belly and hips. He was so careful, so loving, that tears pricked her eyes and she let them. Right then, there was no past, no future, no strings, just her and Owen and the feel of his hands on her skin.

He slowly made his way back up to her breasts, running his soapy hands over her nipples, cupping the firm weight in his palms before using his hands to wash the suds away. When he slid his hands under the water again and between her legs, she let out a moan, parting her thighs for him so he could reach the core of her.

His fingers worked like magic, slowly sliding over her folds and the hood of her clit before coming back up her body for more soap. He worked her up until she was ready to come before he stopped and kissed the side of her neck.

"Turn around for me, Lizzie. I need to get your back."

She opened her eyes lazily. "Hmm?"

Owen smiled softly and kissed her lips. "Straddle me so I can get the rest of you."

Well in that case.

She turned in his arms carefully, aware of the water around them, and slid her legs over his so her core pressed firmly to his cock. They both groaned, but didn't rotate their hips to get closer.

The time hadn't come yet.

But soon.

Oh so soon.

She kept her eyes open this time, their gazes never parting as he slid his hands up and down her back, the scent of peaches in the air was heavy. When his fingers slid between her cheeks, she didn't stiffen. Instead, she leaned forward to give him better access. He slowly worked one finger inside her, then another, the burn intense, but with the water surrounding them, it wasn't as bad as it had been before. Her breasts felt heavy, and her body ached for release. With that in mind, she slowly arched her hips, her clit rubbing along the hard ridge of his cock.

"That's it," he whispered. "Make yourself come that way while I work you to make sure you're ready for me. Can you do that, Liz? Can you come just sliding along my cock?"

She leaned forward and took his lower lip between her teeth in a hard bite before pulling away. "Only with you," she said honestly. "Only with you."

Owen's eyes flared as he worked another finger inside and she called out, her hips working faster as she rubbed on him. With both reactions happening at once, it was too intense, too *much,* and she finally came, her fingers digging into his shoulders.

He slowly released his fingers before kissing her softly. "You're so beautiful when you come. All rosy like a goddess. Ready for bed?"

Her arms felt heavy, the rest of her body even heavier. "I need you inside of me."

"Soon, Lizzie."

Somehow, he got them both out of the tub and toweled off before carrying her into his bedroom. He laid her down over a soft towel on his bed before kissing her slowly, as if he couldn't get enough of her.

"I want you to face me while you do it," she said quickly. "I want to see you."

Owen leaned back and nodded. "Anything you want." He left a kiss on both of her nipples before going back to put on a condom as well as extra lube. She played with her breasts as he worked her again, this time with more lube on his fingers, and she knew that as soon as he was fully inside her, she'd come. He was just so damn good with his hands.

He hovered over her, his body pressing into hers before he kissed her softly. "You ready?"

She arched her hips up and clung to his shoulders. "Yes. Please. We both want this."

He kissed her again, this time pressing forward. The sting burned far more than his fingers, but this wasn't the first time she'd done this in her life so she was prepared for that. However, Owen was bigger than the other man, so she was thankful that they'd been preparing for weeks.

He slowly thrust in and out of her until he was fully seating and sweat covered them both. Though she'd been relaxed after the bath, her body had stiffened again as soon as he entered her.

"You okay?"

She nodded, swallowing hard. "Yeah, you're kind of big, you know."

He smiled softly. "You say the nicest things to me."

Liz reached up to cup his face. "Move. I need you to move. Make us come."

"As my lady commands. But I want you to rub your clit with me at the same time. Can you do that?"

She nodded and slid her hand down her belly and over her core. Her fingers tangled with Owen's as they both rubbed her clit, her pussy so wet it was easy for them to slid over her. He thrust in and out of her, the burn easing into an untold pleasure she'd never felt before.

"You're so fucking tight that I'm not going to last long," Owen panted through gritted teeth.

"I'm almost there, too."

"Come, Liz. Come on my dick."

She thrust her chest forward, and Owen took that as in invitation to suck on her breasts. Between that, their hands on her clit, and the way he moved, she didn't last much longer. She came, her body shaking and her mind going hazy at the intensity of it. Dimly, she felt Owen come, as well, his shout loud enough to wake the other neighbors.

Liz felt as if she came for hours, her body still shaking as Owen pulled out of her fully. The burn came back but before she could cry out, Owen had his mouth between her legs as he licked up the evidence of her arousal. She came again, this time knowing it was too much for her.

She blinked a few times, trying to catch her breath but could only let herself sink into the abyss that they'd sent her to. That Owen had placed her in.

A soft kiss to her lips.

A warm washcloth between her legs.

Strong arms around her.

Another kiss to her neck.

Covers over their bodies.

A soft growl against her skin.

And as she breathed her thanks, her happiness, a soft set of words reached her ears.

"I love you."

But before she could wonder if that was just her imagination or Owen's real words, she fell into slumber, her body far too sated to keep awake...and far too gone for her to wonder if she could say the words back.

Chapter Eleven

Gripping the edge of the porcelain, Liz felt as though she were about to die. Okay, maybe it wasn't as dramatic as all that, but she sure wasn't up to her normal self. Her body ached, and she kept having to throw up. Not the best thing for a nurse to be doing, so they'd sent her home. She couldn't infect the patients, after all.

Yet Liz couldn't help but remember the smug look in Lisa's eyes as Liz had stumbled out of the ER, her head pounding and her stomach queasy. Her job was on the line, and yet there was nothing she could do about it. They'd checked her for a fever, but she'd come up normal so there was nothing they could do for her other than have her lay in a bed and get through whatever stomach bug she had, and she could do that at home. But she had a feeling Lisa and Nancy would be documenting this as yet another mark against her.

And while Liz might be the best at her job in some respects, it would come down to politics in the end since everyone was good at most aspects of their duties. That was a game she'd never been good at, and she was afraid she just might lose this one.

Her stomach rolled, and she heaved over her toilet, emptying the rest of her stomach, though she wasn't sure what else she could purge at this point. Sweat coated her skin, and her brain hurt to work through the fog of dizziness.

She'd come home and headed straight to her bathroom to finish getting sick. She wasn't even sure she'd locked the damn door behind her. It was still early enough in the day that there'd been frost on the lawn and a cold, bitter wind through the rising sun, and yet even that hadn't seemed to cool her off. She might not have an actual fever, but her body felt like it was on fire anyway.

Whatever bug she'd caught, it was *not* the best experience in the world. She needed to somehow find the energy to stand up and put on normal clothes instead of the scrubs she still wore, as well as eat something to settle her stomach. That was if she could even keep anything down. However, she knew she needed to try and at least drink fluids to keep hydrated. The longer this went on, the harder it would be for her to bounce back.

With a sigh, she leaned her head against the wall and closed her eyes. She told herself she'd get up soon. *Soon.*

She'd just about drifted off when she heard the front door open. Tessa was at work and probably hadn't heard that Liz had gone home early, so Liz didn't know whom that could be. She tensed, afraid she'd been an idiot for leaving the door unlocked.

"Liz? The door's unlocked and I saw your car in the driveway as I headed out to work. Where are you? I thought you had an early shift this morning."

Owen's voice soothed her, and she relaxed. He was here and could help her get into bed, or at least make sure she didn't spend the whole day on the bathroom floor. Of course, she didn't want him to see her like this, but she didn't have the energy to worry about that just then. How she'd gone from pushing him away to wanting him near when she wasn't feeling well she didn't know, and it worried her a bit, but for now, she couldn't think too hard about it, not when her pulse pounded a staccato beat in her temples.

"In here," she called out, though her voice was more of a garbled whisper than the shout she'd wanted.

Owen came into the bathroom and frowned. "What's wrong?" He went to his knees and put the back of his hand over her forehead. It was such a protective and caring gesture that a small part of her fell for him all over again. It scared her to no end, but she didn't have the energy to fight it, not then.

"They sent me home," she said softly.

"I can see that. What are your symptoms?" He moved around, and she opened her eyes to watch him pull out a washcloth and dampen it under the faucet.

"Who sounds like they're in the medical field now?"

Owen looked over his shoulder and winked. "Well, nurses and doctors are notoriously bad patients according to TV dramas."

She winced. "If that's your source for the medical field, I'm going to have to disappoint you and tell you that we don't actually have sex in the break rooms. Or storage closets. Or anywhere else. The amount of germs running through the place is disgusting." She looked down at her scrubs and cursed. "And I shouldn't even be wearing these right now because I'm probably spreading things all around."

Owen pressed the cool washcloth to her forehead, and she sighed into him. "We'll just get you out of those right now then. And I've got to say, I'm kind of glad there aren't any shenanigans going on at work. It never seemed very sexy doing it at a hospital."

She tried to smile but failed, her stomach revolting again. This time, Owen held back her hair and ran a hand down her back as she heaved. She should have been embarrassed but couldn't be, not with Owen right there to take care of her. She'd never let anyone— including Tessa—take care of her like this, and yet she couldn't help but let Owen do it. She should have been worried about that, but instead, she leaned into him, promising she'd worry about it later.

She pressed herself to him, and he ran his hand through her hair. "Okay, Liz darling, let's get you out of these scrubs and into something comfy. Then we're getting you into bed, and I'll see what either of us has for upset stomachs."

Liz looked up at him and frowned. "I thought you were off to work."

"You're more important," he said simply. "I'll call the guys and let them know I won't be in today. They can handle one day without me."

Considering he'd been saying the opposite since the day she'd met him, she wasn't sure how she felt about how he dropped everything for her. It should have been too much, and yet...

Her gaze landed on a box over the sink, and she

froze. She closed her eyes, doing mental math, bile once again filling her throat. How could she have been this stupid? She knew the risks, *knew* how to take care of herself, and yet she hadn't done the math.

"What is it?" Owen asked, his voice full of worry as he knelt beside her. "Is something worse? Do I need to take you back to the hospital?"

She shook her head numbly, her gaze still on the box above her. This couldn't be happening. It couldn't. It was just a bug, just a day where she'd get over everything soon and move on. It wasn't what she thought it could be. It wasn't.

"Liz, baby, you're scaring me." He pulled her hair back from her face and moved so he was in her line of sight. "Talk to me."

"I'm late," she croaked out, her words a hoarse whisper.

He frowned, his eyebrows furrowing and that damn ring of his glinting in the light. "What? I don't understand. You were just at work, and you came home. You can't be late."

She shook her head, cursing herself for doing so when her brain went fuzzy again. "I'm *late*," she said again, putting emphasis on the last word.

His eyes widened, but she didn't see the fear she should have there. "Oh." He swallowed hard. "Okay, then." He let out a breath. "And you're feeling sick. Well. I guess the next thing on the list would be for you to take a test to see if that all leads up to one answer or if it's all just coincidence. I can go to the store for you if you want. You'll just need to tell me what kind works best. I'd say we could go to a doctor since those tests are more reliable, right? They use blood? But since you work at a hospital, things might get tricky with the whole privacy thing, and I know how you like to be private about everything in your life. So just help me make a list, and I'll get you all the tests you need. Then we'll do this together." He cupped her face. "We'll do this together," he repeated. "Because I might not be able to throw up for you or pee on a stick, but I can do other things."

Why was he being so sweet? And hell, it was just like Owen to ramble on about lists and organizing things when it came to a freaking *pregnancy test*.

"Owen," she said after a moment. "I...I can't think."

"It's okay. I don't think I'm thinking either. Of course, the fact that I just said think really makes that confusing."

She pressed her lips together, holding back a laugh even though there was nothing to laugh about right then. Not when the one thing she told herself she'd never do might be happening at the worst possible time. He was totally freaking out trying to list his way into calming down. There was no calming down from this.

"There are a couple of tests in the linen closet next to the sink," she said after a moment, her voice oddly toneless. If she didn't feel, didn't put too much into anything, she wouldn't break. Because she was so close to breaking right then, she wasn't sure what she was going to do. She couldn't become her mother, couldn't turn Owen into her father, but once they had a child... Her body shook. Once they had a child, things would change, and she'd become the person she hated the most. She was already not the nicest person in the world because she always pushed people away to protect herself and them, but once that last piece snapped into place, she'd break.

"You have tests in the closet?" Owen asked, confusion on his face once again.

Liz sighed. "Yes. Tessa and I are two single, sexually active women in the medical field. We also have condoms and other options when it comes to protecting our bodies during intercourse with a partner. Yes, we keep pregnancy tests around just in case because sometimes stress makes our periods late and that can be a trying time. This will just be that time." She let out a breath. "But we need to be sure."

"We will be," he said after a moment and stood up to

rummage through her linen closet. His hands didn't shake, and he seemed so sure of himself. Yet she knew he was freaking out inside. Probably not as much as she was, but enough that he was running on autopilot.

She pressed her fingers over her eyes, willing herself to snap out of it and not go numb. She needed to take this test, find out it was negative, and eat some crackers to settle her stomach. They'd been safe each and every time they'd had sex. There hadn't been a single accident, tear in the condom, or time where he'd accidentally entered her before pulling out. Even when he'd sent her into a sex-induced coma, they'd been safe.

And yet she knew condoms weren't a hundred percent effective.

Her body shook. Tessa and others were lucky that they could also have other birth control to protect themselves, but Liz could only use condoms. It wasn't inevitable that she'd have this...occurrence, but the math didn't lie.

"You have two kinds here," Owen said as he sank back onto the floor next to her holding two boxes. "One has the lines on it, the other a clear readout. Which one do you want first?"

"First?" She clearly wasn't running on all cylinders at the moment.

"I assumed you'd want to take it twice to be sure."

He was being so careful with her, as if afraid she'd snap at any moment. And she knew he wasn't wrong in that assessment.

She let out a breath. "The clear readout first, then. I could use easy wording."

"Gotcha." He opened the box and handed over a foil-covered stick. "The instructions are right on the box. I read them already just in case, but it should only take three minutes after you pee on the applicator for the words to show up. I won't stand in here and watch you take it, but I'll get you a glass of water or something if you need it." He sighed and cupped her face. She didn't lean into his touch like she had been doing recently, and they both noticed but didn't say anything. "I'll be right outside that door. You call me when you need me inside." He shook his head. "Or rather, when it's time to read the test."

Because she wouldn't admit that she needed him.

Damn it, he knew her so well, and it killed her that she was hurting him, and yet, if that test ended up positive, she knew she'd hurt him even more. That's how things like this worked. It might not be logical to others, but it made sense to her in some twisted way.

"I could use water for the second test," she said after a moment.

"Okay, then." He kissed her softly, and she pulled back.

"I just threw up."

"I can handle a little vomit," he said with a wink, though the humor didn't reach his eyes.

"But this is probably just a stomach bug that you caught." They both knew it might not be a stomach bug.

"Then I get sick, and you get to play doctor with me again. Be right back." He stood up and left her alone in the bathroom, closing the door behind him.

Knowing she could only stare at the foil-covered stick for so long without making herself go crazy, she stood up and unwrapped the thing, reading the instructions on the pamphlet inside the box, as well.

Two minutes later, she had the test on the counter, and Owen had come back in to watch the words appear with her.

Three minutes after that, her world shattered.

"We're pregnant," Owen said in shocked awe. "Holy...okay, then."

She blinked, everything around her moving in slow motion though her heart raced, pounding so hard she was afraid it would leap right out of her chest. Some small part of her had actually hoped that it would be negative and that everything had just been a sad coincidence. That's how it needed to be.

Because she could *not* be pregnant.

She could *not* be a mother.

He turned her in his arms, cupping her face once again. "You're not saying anything. I know you're shocked, and hell, so am I. Hence why I'm rambling on like this. But, yeah, we're pregnant, Liz. Pregnant."

"Stop saying that," she rasped.

He blinked. "What?"

"Stop saying that word," she bit out. "I can't think right now, Owen. I can barely breathe, and you keep saying that word over and over again as if trying to make it real." She was honestly losing it right now, and she couldn't help herself as she fell down the rabbit hole.

Owen leaned back, his hands falling as she pulled away. "It *is* real, Liz. Do you need to sit down? Are you feeling ill again?"

She fisted her hands at her sides. "All my life, I've done everything I could to gain the control I lost as a child. *Everything*. Now, I might lose my job, I'm in a relationship I wanted to stay away from, and now...and now I'm..." She laughed, but it was a hollow sound that made her tear up. "I can't even say the word, Owen. I need some space, okay? I can't think with you around. Everything gets jumbled."

Owen stood straight, his face a mask. "I see."

But he didn't see. He couldn't. Not when she couldn't see herself.

"I just need some space to think."

"Well, when you're in that space, I want you to think about this. The relationship you didn't want to be in? Well, we're in it, Liz. You and I were moving toward something I thought we both wanted, and hell, now we're smack in the middle of it. You haven't pushed me away in weeks, not the way you did when you were scared at the start of it, so you don't get to use that excuse. You're scared now, and I get that. Fuck, I'm scared, too, but I'm not going anywhere in the grand scheme of things. I'll leave now so you can breathe, but I'm going to be close, because, Liz? I love you. I love you so fucking much it hurts, and I want to spend the rest of my life with you. And, yeah, by the way you're paling even more right now—though I didn't think that was possible since you've been sick—I get that you don't want to hear that. But, yeah, I love you. I was waiting to say it when you were ready. And maybe now isn't the best time, standing in a bathroom after you were just throwing up, feeling as if our worlds have shifted. But I love you."

"You can't," she whispered. "I'm no good for you, Owen. I..." He pressed his finger to her lips.

"Don't tell me what I feel. I get that you're scared,

and with what you grew up with? Yeah, I get it. So I'm going to let you have your space today because I don't want to push you more than you already feel pushed. But I want you to promise me something." He let out a shaky breath. "Don't...don't do anything about this until we talk okay?" His voice broke at the end, and she blinked back tears.

Her heart thudded, pain radiating through her at the thought of ending the life growing inside her. "Oh, Owen. I would never...I would *never* take out your rights or choices." She pressed her lips together. "I just can't think with you around, but my needing space has nothing to do with wanting you away so I can do something we would both regret."

He visibly shuddered before moving forward and kissing her forehead. "Thank you," he whispered. "I love you, Liz. And I'm going to keep saying it until you believe me. Now I'm going to go so you can breathe, but I'm coming back. I'll always come back."

As she watched him walk away, she finally let the tears fall. She had no idea what she was doing other than she knew she needed time to think, time to breathe.

She honestly had no idea what she wanted or what she was going to do, and yet she was so afraid that, one day, she'd push him away hard enough that he wouldn't come back.

And then...well, then she wasn't sure what the answer was.

Because she was pregnant, and there was no denying that. Now she just needed to figure out what that meant because she couldn't become her mother. She couldn't hate the life growing inside her.

She wouldn't.

No matter what.

And that meant she needed to figure out how to become the woman she wanted to be, rather than the one she was painfully aware she might become.

Owen had thought the day he found out he would be a father would be a day of celebration. He loved his niece and nephew, as well as the Montgomery kids that always seemed to be around and called him their honorary uncle. He'd known that he wanted to be a father one day, a husband, a family man, and as he'd spent more and more time with Liz, he'd known the woman he wanted to spend the rest of his life with was her.

Only she didn't want to spend hers with him.

Or, at least, that's what she was saying right then.

"Want to tell us why you look like you want to

punch something and at the same time throw up?" Murphy asked as he sank down onto the couch next to him.

Owen turned at his brother's voice and noticed how pale he looked. "You doing okay?"

Murphy shrugged. "Just long hours on that project, but I should be done soon. And stop worrying about me, Mother Hen. I thought Graham was the one who worried about all of us."

"I am," Graham said as he entered the living room. "But Jake and Owen are allowed to pitch in when I'm not around. It's how big brothers work. And you do look a little pale, little brother. Eat something." He handed over a tray of stuffed mushrooms, and Murphy rolled his eyes before grabbing a couple.

Owen had called Graham right as he'd left Liz's to say that he needed to talk but hadn't mentioned what about. He had spent the day alone in his house, working on lists and plans for work rather than dealing with his life that felt like it was spiraling out of control. Graham had insisted that Owen come over for dinner, and the rest of the Gallagher crew had shown up—minus Rowan, who was at a friend's house—to make sure he was okay. Noah was asleep in the portable crib they'd set up in the guest room, and the rest of them were now in the living room, ready for Owen to speak.

"Tell us what's up," Maya said as she perched on Border's lap. "Did you and Liz have a fight?"

Owen set his glass of water down on the table, his mind already too fuzzy for him to even think of drinking.

"Liz is pregnant."

Everyone was silent for a moment before they all started talking at once. Blake and Maya rushed over to hug him as the guys pounded him on the back, saying congratulations and wondering where Liz was.

He pulled away, resting his head in his hands as people went back to their seats. "Liz...Liz said she needed some space to think about things."

Murphy turned and put his hand on Owen's shoulder. "What kinds of things?"

Owen let out a shaky breath, knowing he was close to breaking down in front of his family. They wouldn't taunt him for it, but he needed to tell them what he could before he broke down. He also couldn't betray Liz's confidence and tell them about her past in full.

"Liz grew up..." He shook his head. "I can't tell you everything because it's not my story to tell, but let's just say her life wasn't easy growing up."

"And now she's about to have a child in a relationship where she probably spent most of it second-guessing herself," Border put in.

Owen lifted his head, surprised at the clarity with which Border spoke.

"Don't be so shocked," Border said softly. "I don't like to speak unless it's important, though you Gallaghers and Montgomerys are slowly working on that. But you guys know I grew up with a shitty parent who made me think that I didn't deserve what I had. And when Maya found out she was pregnant?" He shook his head. "Scared the shit out of me. I didn't think I was good enough for her and Jake, and I almost ruined what we had because of it."

"And we understood," Jake put in. "But we didn't back down."

"We're stubborn like that," Maya added. "And you're pretty stubborn yourself, Owen. Give her time to think because surprise pregnancies are scary as hell, but don't leave her alone completely. She needs to know you're there." She paused. "You *will* be there, right?"

Owen nodded. "I love her, damn it. Of course, I want to be there. I'm *going* to be here."

Blake spoke next, her voice softer than usual. "Give her the space she needs like Maya said, but don't back away. We don't know her past, but I did my best to push away Graham because I was scared, and I have a feeling Liz might be in the same boat."

"I pushed you away, too," Graham added, his voice gruff. "And I regret that."

Blake looked over at her husband and smiled. "It's okay. We both made mistakes, but we're here now. Together." She looked back at Owen. "It's hard work to make any relationship work, and when someone has extra heavy baggage, it just makes it that much harder. But I know you, Owen. You're not going to back down."

"I won't. I just hate that I can't seem to get through to her."

"You seemed to be getting through just fine before this," Murphy said after a moment. "You're persistent like any decent Gallagher." They all let out a soft laugh. "But, Owen? Think about this. You're here, talking with us, knowing you have a kick-ass support system. Liz? She has Tessa. That's it. And while Tessa is strong as hell and can help Liz, she's going to need more than just her best friend. We all do."

Owen narrowed his eyes at his baby brother. "You're a lot more insightful than we give you credit for."

His eyes darkened for a moment before he blinked the look away, a lazy smile crossing his lips. "Well, women like me. What can I say?"

"So you keep telling yourself," Maya added dryly. "Okay, Owen. Just know we're here for you. And Liz, too. Because we like her, you know. She's good for you, even if she is totally not who I thought you'd end up with."

Jake laughed. "Yeah, I thought he'd end up with a sweet, quiet woman who would probably get scared off by the lot of us."

"There's always hope for Murphy that he'll find a quiet woman since the rest of us didn't seem to manage that."

Both Blake and Maya flipped him off.

Owen smiled and leaned back into the couch, finally starting to relax since the moment he'd seen Liz on the floor in pain. She'd pushed him away and looked so fucking scared about being pregnant, but hell, he was scared, too. And while she might think she didn't need him, didn't want a relationship, her actions for the past weeks had gone against that.

He'd give her time, then he'd figure out a way to show her that they could work. That she wouldn't turn into her mother. Because, damn it, she wasn't anything like the shrew she'd described. She was caring, sweet when she wanted to be, and put everyone else before herself. Hence why she'd tried to break things off before —to protect *him*, not her.

He loved her, and he wasn't going to give up on her. And...

"I'm going to be a father," he whispered. "A *father*."

Murphy patted his knee. "Just now getting to you, huh?"

Owen blinked, his heart racing. "I need to make lists. Get ready. I don't know how to be a dad."

His family cracked up, and he laughed with them, his mind going in a thousand different directions. He told himself everything would be okay. Because it had to be. *It has to be.*

Chapter Twelve

"You're a damn mess," Tessa proclaimed as she walked into Liz's room. "A fucking mess, who needs to get her head on straight."

Liz glared at Tessa's reflection in the mirror. "Nice words coming from you." She winced at how hard she sounded. She shouldn't be attacking Tessa at all. "Sorry."

"Don't be. I know you don't mean it. I'm the easiest person to lash out at when you're scared, and I have thick skin. Plus, I do the same to you. That's why we're friends."

"I need to get ready for work, Tessa. I took yesterday off to throw up for hours, but now I can't take any more time off. They're announcing the budget and the ramifi-

229

cations today, and I can't be late, nor can I just not show up because I'm freaking out."

Tessa ran her hand down her pencil skirt and shook her head. "You shouldn't have anything to worry about since you're the best nurse they have."

"Well, I'm also the one who hasn't sucked up enough. Everyone else seems to have someone they can kiss up to. I don't have anyone like that."

"Because you focus on your patients and the work that goes with the job."

Liz's body felt like she'd run a marathon, her muscles ached, and not just because of the pregnancy. She'd been working far harder than usual with everything going on, and her body was starting to feel it more and more.

"It's exhausting, Tessa," she said softly. "I'm just so sick of it all."

Tessa met Liz's eyes in the mirror again. "Then what are you going to do about it?"

Liz studied her friend's face again before shaking her head. "I don't know. Keep working, I guess. It's what I'm good at."

Tessa pressed her lips together, folding her arms over her crisp blouse. "And Owen? What are you going to do about him? Because, frankly, he's the best thing that's ever happened to you, and I hate that you keep running away from him. You guys are going to have a freaking baby, and he's not here because he's doing as you asked and giving you space. I give him props for staying away as long as he has so far. Because, hell, those Gallaghers don't like to be pushed around."

Just the sound of Owen's name made Liz's pulse race, but she wasn't sure if it was because she still wanted him by her side or that she was ashamed of how she'd acted. She hated that she'd said the things she did and had put that fear into his eyes about the baby. She just wasn't good at dealing with things and ended up harming more than she wanted to.

Just like her mother.

"I don't know what I'm doing there either," she admitted. "But I can't do everything at once, damn it. Let me get through today and whatever the job entails before I figure out the rest."

"First, doing things in order like that never works out for you. It's all layered and connected and gets in the way of things. Second, you can't keep blaming yourself for what your mother did. You are not your mother, and you know this. You *know* this. So stop getting on that one-way track where you end up circling back to thinking that everything you do means you're going to break like she did."

"I don't know what else do to," Liz said after a moment. "It's all I know."

"That's a silly answer," Tessa snapped. "Grow up and be your own person, because you're growing a damn person, and I want to be fun aunt Tessa. So don't fuck this up. Owen needs you. Just as much as you need him."

And with that, Tessa stomped away, muttering under her breath and leaving Liz once again alone with her vicious thoughts. She needed to get to work and just get this over with, but her mind kept going back to Owen.

What was she going to do?

With every passing thought, every passing moment, the idea that she was going to have a baby became more and more real. And that scared her.

Plenty of women were terrified at the thought of having a baby the first few weeks after they found out they were pregnant, so she was not alone in thinking the way she was, but it still shamed her that she couldn't just jump on board. There was truly something wrong with her, and yet she didn't have time to dwell on that.

She had to focus on going to work right then and fighting for her job.

If she had a job at all after the day was through, that was.

. . .

Tension rode thick throughout the ER that morning, but Liz shoved it away, focusing on her patients that needed her more than errant thoughts of what was to come. The day hadn't been that busy so far, but there was no way she was going to say something like that aloud. It was bad enough to taunt the gods by even thinking it.

She was just finishing up some paperwork when Nancy came into the nursing station, a bland look on her face. "Liz? I need you to come with me."

Liz froze before carefully setting down the chart she'd just finished updating. "To the break room?" she asked, aware that was where Nancy had taken the past two nurses to tell them that their job was safe. Apparently, Nancy was having fun letting each and every person know in private about the state of their position at the hospital.

If Liz weren't freaking out over so many things, she could really start to hate this woman more than she already did. After rolling her shoulders, she followed Nancy back to the break room. She'd know soon enough what her future held, and she knew she'd just have to get through it no matter what. Everything seemed to be falling from her grasp, and she couldn't quite find her footing, but she knew she was good at her job. She had the highest performance evaluations of the floor and worked longer hours than most because she didn't have a family to go home to, not to mention that she honestly wanted to make sure others were taken care of. She had to trust in her ability to do what she did best: help people.

Surely, the people upstairs would understand that.

Nancy didn't bother taking a seat at a table; instead, she went directly to the coffee maker to pour herself a cup. She didn't bother to offer Liz one.

"As you know, the budget committee finally agreed on a final budget for the year this morning," Nancy began.

"I've heard." It was all anyone could talk about, even though they had numerous other things to worry about.

"Well, then you've also heard that there have been changes on each floor, not just the ER itself. None of it was personal, of course, but business is business."

"I thought this was a hospital where the business was to ensure that people made it out of these doors alive," Liz put in, her tone grating. She hated being talked down to like she was a child, and Nancy excelled at it.

The other woman raised her brow. "Be that as it may, some decisions had to be made, and unfortunately, you are on the upper tier in terms of salary.

You've been with us the longest in your position, and as there isn't another position higher than you opening up, that means the committee had to make tough decisions.

A ringing sound buzzed in Liz's ears as she tried to make sense of what she was hearing. "You're saying I make too much money because I've been here longer than anyone else, and that since you're in the position higher than me and haven't moved up yet,"—because Nancy couldn't seem to get promoted herself, but Liz didn't say that—"I'm what? Going to get a salary cut?" She barely made enough as it was with all her loans and the new house. And now that she was pregnant, things were going to change dramatically.

Nancy shook her head. "That wouldn't be enough, sadly. The board, as well as the committee, has been forced into this position, and in order to help the hospital stay afloat, you're being let go. You have two more weeks, of course, to gather your things and make plans, but then that's it. This decision didn't come easily, but really, it's the best for everyone involved." Nancy reached out and patted Liz's hand. "You didn't really fit in here anyway, did you, darling? You'll be better off somewhere else, don't you think?"

Liz snatched back her hand as if she'd been scalded. What the fuck was this woman thinking? "You've got to be kidding me. I've worked here the longest and have the best record so I get fired because I don't make nice?"

Nancy raised her chin. "Honey, don't make a scene. You must have known this was coming. And, really, you don't have as good a record as you think. What with dating patients like you are, and leaving early yesterday. If you truly cared about your job, you would have worked harder."

Liz fisted her hands at her sides. "That's bull, and we both know it. I don't kiss your ass like Lisa does, and I get that, but that doesn't mean I should be fired. And as for dating patients? You and Lisa have been the ones spreading that around, so don't fuck with me on that. My personal life is my own business."

"Not when it's the hospital's business," Nancy cut in.

"Fuck you, Nancy. You and Lisa wanted me out, and you found a way to make that happen. And I left yesterday because I was sick, not because I needed a mani-pedi. You know what? Maybe you're right. Maybe I didn't fit in with you and your clique, but I worked my ass off, and now I'm being thrown out because you don't like me and found a way to make your dreams come true. Well, really, fuck you again, Nancy. I have over two weeks vacation left, and I'm taking it. I'm out, and you get to pay me for it for those last two weeks. Fight me on it, and I'll come at you with everything I have. And believe me, *honey*, it's enough."

With that, she stormed out of the break room and back to her cubby where she stored her things. She was done with the place and the long hours and low pay. She'd worked her ass off for everything she'd achieved, and now she had nothing to show for it because she didn't get along with the woman in charge.

Fuck all of them.

Her hands shook as she stuffed her duffle bag with the remnants of her locker. Holy God. She'd just been fired. She didn't have a job. She would lose her insurance at the exact wrong time, as well.

What the hell was she going to do?

Lisa walked by at that moment and giggled. Fucking giggled. Liz turned on her heel and glared at the woman. "Just go away, Lisa. You got what you wanted. But remember this, the patients need to come first. Got it? Don't let someone die because you're too busy gloating and being a bitch."

"Go to hell, Liz. Maybe if you hadn't gotten all high and mighty, you wouldn't have been tossed out on your ass." With that, she flounced away, and Liz was left shaking.

"Liz?"

She turned as Dr. Wilder came up to her, his hands

in his jeans' pockets. He looked like he was about to head off shift, and Liz wanted nothing more than to just walk away and never turn back. She didn't have the energy to deal with any of this.

But she couldn't be a bitch to the man who actually put patients first before all other things—including himself and those he worked with.

"Yes?"

"I just wanted to say I'm sorry. I know it doesn't mean much, but I put in a good word for you, but Nancy has a way of getting what she wants." He narrowed his eyes. "I'm going to make sure she can't do this to anyone else, though. I was just a little late this time in seeing her for who she is, and for that I'm sorry." He pulled out a card from his pocket and handed it over. "I know you're not ready to think about this, but my brother has a clinic that could always use the help." He shrugged as she took it, her eyes wide.

"Why are you doing this?"

"Because you're the best nurse we have, and we're losing you to silly politics. Don't let your gift go to waste because other people are assholes."

She shook her head before looking down at the card. "An oncology outpatient clinic?"

"I know it's not an ER, but they will have better hours for you and the baby."

Her head shot up. "What?"

He gave her a small smile. "I've been a doctor for a while now, Liz. I can recognize the signs of a pregnant woman, even if she can't herself. Congratulations, by the way. And if you need a reference for anything, just let me know."

And with that, he gave her a nod before heading out, leaving her confused as ever. People surprised her every day, and yet with her world falling out from under her feet, she didn't know what to think.

What the hell was she supposed to do now?

Owen stepped into the house as Tessa answered the door. "How is she?" he asked, his palms sweaty.

"Freaking out and alternating between cleaning things and getting sick in the bathroom. Right now, I think she's sitting on the bed trying not to get nauseous." Tessa gave him a look he couldn't decipher. "Thanks for coming over as quickly as you did."

Tessa had called him at the jobsite, and he'd dropped everything to come to Liz. His brothers had once again understood, and he couldn't help but feel grateful. He still felt like he was messing things up at work with everything going on, but he needed to put Liz first.

"I'm always going to be here for her," Owen said quickly. "No matter what."

Tessa smiled then, her eyes brightening. "I actually believe you, and that makes my cold Grinch heart warm. Now, go make her feel like a queen that can take on the world. But at the same time, don't do so much that she has a panic attack and runs away again."

Owen couldn't help the snort that escaped. "You sound like you've done this often."

"She does the same for me. It's why we're best friends."

"Sisters more like."

A weird look passed over Tessa's face as she nodded. "Yeah. Sisters." She cleared her throat. "Anyway, go get her. I'll be in my room if you need me."

Owen gave her arm a squeeze before heading back to the bedroom to check on Liz. She hadn't exactly invited him over, but he knew she had to be hurting, and he couldn't leave her alone.

When he'd made it to the end of the hallway, he found her sitting cross-legged in the middle of the bed, rolling her head over her shoulders. From the lemon smell that hit his senses, he knew she'd been scrubbing down the whole place for some time, and he was just happy that she was functional enough to do that. She'd drawn in on herself before, and he'd been afraid for her, so he had to count this as progress.

"Liz." He didn't want to frighten her since her eyes were closed.

She turned to him, opening her eyes and letting out a breath. "Tessa called you."

"Yeah, she did." He slowly walked into the room and sat down on the bed next to her. He gave her space so they weren't touching, but he could still feel the heat of her. Damn, he loved this woman, every prickly inch of her, and he understood why she felt the need to be so independent. He just hoped she'd give him a chance.

"I lost my job today." She didn't look at him as she spoke, but reached over and took his hand.

He swallowed hard and threaded his fingers with hers. "I know. I'm sorry, hon. They made a mistake. A big one."

Liz surprised the hell out of him by scooting over and leaning her head on his shoulder. "Yeah, they did." A pause. "I'm sorry for being a bitch and kicking you out yesterday. I couldn't think straight, and having you near always messes with my brain." She squeezed his hand. "In a good way, usually. Sorry. That didn't come out right." She sighed. "I'm so not good at this."

He kissed the top of her head. "I'm pretty new at

this, too, you know, so I'm not good at it either. It's okay, we'll work on it together." Together. He liked the sound of that.

"I don't know what I'm going to do, Owen. This just sucks."

He used his other hand to rub small circles on her knee. "I know it sucks. But you're a strong person with a great record and damn good at what you do. You'll find a job soon that's perfect for you, one where you don't have to jump through hoops because other people are so insecure they can't see what's right in front of their faces."

She leaned back to smile up at him. "You're good with the pep talks."

Daringly, he lowered his head and brushed a kiss over her lips. When she didn't pull back, he counted that as a win. "I wanted to say something like how I wanted to kick their asses, but I didn't."

She snorted and went back to leaning on his shoulder. "When you came in that first night, I was so afraid we'd lose you. I know you weren't injured that severely, but I had this sudden feeling that the world would lose an amazing guy. A guy who I totally couldn't have and should stay away from."

"I was damn lucky you were my nurse." He was damn lucky for a lot of reasons. Least of which that the truck that had hit him hadn't been going that fast. The police still had no leads, but no one seemed to think Owen was in any danger of being attacked again. It was just one of those freak accidents that happened late at night in a bar parking lot.

"I don't know what to do," she repeated.

"You've only been at this for a few hours, Liz. You don't need a plan right now."

"Says the man with four plans going on at once and probably already has a list concerning the baby."

He bit his lip. "Two."

She pulled back, her eyes wide. "We are *not* having twins."

He shook his head, a laugh bubbling out of him. "I meant I have two lists so far. But I will totally throw them out if you want to work on a list from scratch with me." He was treading on thin ice right then, but she had been the one to bring up the baby so that had to count for something.

She swallowed hard before squeezing his hand. "I don't know what the answers are, Owen. I don't know if I'm ready for this, but...but I'd like to look at those lists of yours." Tears slid down her cheeks, and he reached over to brush them away. "I hate crying, and it's all I seem to do with you."

He shook his head and leaned down to kiss the dampness on her cheeks. "It's not all you do." He was doing his best not to throw his fists in the air in triumph at the thought of her wanting to see his lists. This was progress, and it mattered a whole lot more than she thought.

"I guess."

"What do you need me to do right now, Liz? We have time to worry about everything else around us, but right now, let me know what you need."

She blinked up at him, the strength he always saw in her a full force in her eyes. "Hold me? I just need you to hold me."

His heart thudded, and he opened his arms. She crawled into his lap, and he held her close, her body so small compared to his. "Always, Liz. I will *always* hold you."

This is the first step, he thought, and damn if it wasn't a far greater one than he imagined he'd get that night. He'd take this, and when she was ready, they'd take the next step together. Because Owen had to believe in that; had to believe in the next few steps. It was the only way he could manage. The woman in his arms was his future—he just had to make her see that.

Chapter Thirteen

"Why did I say yes to a Gallagher dinner?" Liz asked, tugging on the bottom of her top. She'd decided to wear comfy slacks and a cute sweater instead of a dress, but she still didn't feel like she was doing the right thing.

"Because you like me and my family, and the group of us is finally able to get together to have a family dinner for Rowan's birthday." Owen put his arms around her as they stood on Graham's porch before heading inside and then leaned down to kiss her softly. She melted into him, too lost to care that she'd never wanted to fall so fast, so hard. He was just...*Owen* and there was nothing better most days than having his arms around her.

"Are you sure we didn't need to bring a gift? Or

something for the meal?" She hated coming empty-handed. And since she didn't have a job any longer, she'd had all day to do something for the dinner they'd had planned for weeks, in between her wallowing.

The idea that she'd been fired hadn't fully sunk in yet, even if she'd gone through the wide array of emotions throughout the day. It had only been a short twenty-four hours, after all. She hadn't been sure she had the energy to come to this dinner after being sick in the morning and dealing with the fallout of losing her job, but she and Owen had planned on coming before they'd found out about the baby. And now, according to him, everyone knew he'd knocked her up and they hadn't made a decision about it. And while the idea that so many knew her business might have annoyed her on any other day, she couldn't help but feel a little jealous that he had people to go to when he couldn't think on his own and needed a sounding board.

She reminded herself that she had Tessa. Her best friend had been her everything for years, and Liz would do well to remember that. She might not have a family she could count on, or other friends she could bring in close, but she had Tessa.

And if he had his way, she'd have Owen, as well.

One step at a time, Liz. Just one step at a time.

Owen tapped her on the nose, bringing her out of her spiraling thoughts. "You psyching yourself out yet?"

"No, I had a good freak-out going." She leaned forward to rest her forehead on his shoulder, and he tugged her close.

"I'll let you get back to that after dinner if you want. But first, to answer your question, no, we didn't need to bring anything. Blake and Graham have everything covered and wouldn't let us bring side dishes or desserts to this one. Sometimes, we pitch in; other times, we just go with whatever the host wants. It all depends on what's going on. And I already got Rowan a gift for her actual birthday."

Liz smiled up at him. "That pink and gold planner, right?" God, that was just so like him to get a little girl a daily planner.

He winked. "Yep, it's a mid-year so she can't use it for a couple months, but I also got her stationery and the colored pens I love that write smoothly without smearing. I figured it's never too early to learn how to organize your day."

She snorted, lifting her head so she could kiss his jaw. "You're a dork."

"Your dork," he replied like he always did.

"Are you guys gonna keep kissing on the porch, or

do you want to come in? You're welcome to kiss in here, I guess. That way, you don't get cold."

Liz turned at the sound of Rowan's voice and held back a smile. She hadn't even heard the door open, but apparently, she'd been so lost in Owen, she hadn't cared.

Owen gripped Liz's chin just then and turned her toward him so he could lay a smacking kiss on her lips. "Okay, kissed her. I guess we can come in because I think a certain niece of mine is in dire need of hugs and kisses."

Rowan's eyes widened, and she giggled before turning on her heel and tearing off in the other direction.

Owen looked over his shoulder and winked at Liz. "If you'll excuse me, I have a little girl to catch." He moved quickly after Rowan, making growling sounds as the little girl giggled away.

"It's good to see her laughing like that," Graham said softly as he held out a hand. "Come in from the porch, Liz, and I'll take your coat."

She handed it to him and frowned. "What do you mean? About the laughing?"

He hung up her coat before stuffing his hands into the pockets of his dark jeans. "Rowan isn't technically mine. You know that, right?"

She nodded. "Owen said she was Blake's from a previous relationship but you adopted her recently."

His eyes shone with pride at that last part, and she knew that every child in this family was loved and cared for by these big, burly men and powerful women. She barely kept herself from putting her hand over her stomach, wondering what her child would be like in this family...if they would be enough if she weren't.

"Her birth father's parents weren't happy about Blake raising her and tried to take her from us at one point. It's a big, messy story, but they broke a few laws and scared the shit out of all of us."

Liz's eyes widened as she looked over at Rowan, who was currently being held upside down by Owen as Murphy tickled her into hysterical laughter. "I had no idea."

"Most people don't, and we want to keep it that way. Rowan deserves a normal childhood from here on out, and we're going to do that for her. But, you're family now, so you should know. Owen can give you the details later if you want."

Family. He thought she was family?

"Graham...I don't know where Owen and I are going. Things are still tenuous right now."

He gave her a look that spoke volumes. "You're carrying a Gallagher in there." He nodded at her stomach. "You two might not be married, and hell, you might decide to make a mistake and call it quits with my brother, but you'll always be connected to us because of that child. Now, I'm not going to tell you what to do—"

"Yeah you are," Liz cut in, her voice low. "But do continue."

Graham snorted. "Yeah, you'll fit in with Blake and Maya for sure. But what I was going to say was, do what you need to do for yourself, I get that. If you don't love him, then fine. Don't be in a relationship. Don't hurt him because you're trying to be something you're not. But I don't think that's the case here. I think you're scared. And speaking as someone who almost let the best thing in my life slip through my hands because I was too scared to do something about it, just take some time and think about what you truly want."

Liz studied the man who had a larger beard than Owen and a lot more ink and tried to wonder what he was getting at.

"Do you want me to stay away from Owen? Or get closer? Because I'm not sure exactly which way you want me to go right now."

"I want you to be happy. Same as I want for my brother." Graham shrugged. "But it doesn't really matter what I want. You two are adults that are going to do what is best for the two of you and the life you're carrying. I just wanted you to know that if you decide that Owen is a man you could love, you'll get a whole family in the process. And, if you go the other way, well...we'll still be connected, so you're going to have to get used to us."

She honestly had no idea what to say. She'd never been in a serious relationship before, and as hard as she'd tried to fight it, she and Owen were definitely serious. They had been even before she found out they were pregnant. If she wanted to keep her head on straight and do right by their child, she needed to figure out what she wanted. Because if she didn't soon, she was afraid she'd screw up everything, exactly like she'd been trying to avoid for so many years.

"Everything okay here?" Owen asked as he walked over. He slid his arm around Liz's waist, pulling her to his side.

Graham met Liz's gaze, and she knew she'd have to be the one to speak up. "Everything's fine," she said honestly. He hadn't done anything to her other than say she would be welcomed with open arms if she chose. He'd also asked her not to hurt his little brother, and that was something she was trying to avoid with all of her heart.

Owen glared at Graham, so she turned in his arms and kissed his neck. "Really, Owen. We're good. He's just growly. And I think that's just how Graham talks."

Blake came over at that point and snorted. "You've got that right. He can't help but be a Growly Gus."

Graham narrowed his eyes at his wife. "What did I say about calling me that?"

Blake blinked innocently. "That you love it. Because if you didn't, I wouldn't do that thing you like." She'd whispered that last part since Rowan was in the room, but the little girl was currently wrestling on the floor with Jake and Border. These guys sure loved their niece, and Liz knew that no matter what happened, the child within her would be loved and cared for.

That meant something.

Graham was retreating with his wife as Owen pulled her aside to cup her face. "You're really okay?" he asked.

"Yeah," she said softly. "I'm really okay. He loves you, you know. Like really loves you. They all do. You have no idea how lucky you are." She swallowed the ball of emotion in her throat, aware they had an audience.

"Yeah, Lizzie. I know how lucky I am. I have you."

"Aww, big brother, I didn't know you could be so sweet." Murphy wrapped his arms around Liz and picked her up, forcing a shocked gasp from her lips.

"Put me down!" she called out with a laugh, but he didn't listen.

"I haven't had a chance to say hello," the other man pouted.

"So you're going to throw me around like a bag of potatoes."

"Very gently, of course." He winked, and she lost it, laughter erupting from her.

This family kept tying knots around her. It was as if they knew if they didn't find a way to keep her close, she'd bolt. At least, that's how she'd been wired in the past. Now, though...now she wasn't so sure.

Maybe, just maybe, she could be happy.

By the time the party ended and Liz and Owen were on their way home, Liz was exhausted and in need of a nap. Owen drove so she could lean her head against the seat and nod off.

He had one hand on hers with the other on the steering wheel as she dozed. "You feeling okay?" he asked when they were almost to their street.

She opened her eyes lazily. "Yeah, I am. Thankfully, I don't get carsick right now though that could happen throughout the first trimester."

Owen nodded. "I read that."

She grinned. "Already reading up?"

He smiled widely. "Well, since you're a nurse, you have a leg up on me, so I thought I'd better catch up."

"I don't know everything about childbirth and pregnancy, you know. We don't get as many births in the ER as TV tends to suggest."

"Then we'll learn together," he said simply.

She let out a breath as she studied him, in awe that he could be so calm right now when she was anything but. "Yeah, we can learn together." She could take this chance, she thought. Owen was worth it, worth more. She trusted him with everything she had, and because of that, she knew that maybe one day she could trust herself.

When they pulled into his driveway, his phone buzzed, and he frowned. "Hold on, let me answer that on the cell rather than Bluetooth."

She nodded and stayed where she was, content not to have to get out of the vehicle yet.

"Oh, crap. You doing okay? No, I get it. I'll be right over to pick you up and get you home. No, don't bother calling a cab. You're one of us, man. Yeah. Okay. I'll be there soon." Owen hung up and frowned.

"What's wrong?" she asked. "Is someone hurt?"

He shook his head. "One of the new guys from the jobsite got food poisoning and went to the ER. Not the one you used to work at, but the hospital by his house. His family is out of town on a school trip, and he doesn't have anyone else to pick him up since they just moved here."

"And they won't release him without someone to watch over him." She nodded. "It must have been a pretty severe case but not enough to warrant admission."

"You'd know better than I." He blew out a breath. "I could call someone else, but I don't know who could really get out there at this time."

"It's really okay. Take care of him. I'm just going to take a bath before I go to bed anyway. I have to start making plans tomorrow about what I'm going to do job wise, so I want a good night's sleep."

Owen turned in his seat and kissed her softly. "I'm going to miss seeing you in the bath."

She grinned. "You can see me tomorrow when I take a bath to relieve all the stress from planning. You might like making lists and charts, and yeah, I do—a little—but this time, it might be too much for one day."

"You'll call if you need me? Tonight or tomorrow?"

She kissed him hard on the lips. "I will." The fact that she'd said that so readily without feeling caged told her how far she'd come with him. She was falling for him day by day and knew that soon there would be no turning back.

And she wasn't sure if she wanted that option at all anymore, anyway.

Liz kissed him one more time before heading toward her house, her mind on the things she had to do the next day to find a job. She'd let herself wallow for over a day, and now it was time to make plans for her future. Blended within that was her relationship with Owen, but that didn't scare her as much as it used to.

She was just about to head to the bath when her doorbell rang. She frowned, wondering if it was Owen. They hadn't exchanged keys yet because they were always over at each other's houses anyway, and if she were honest, she'd kept that boundary up because she was scared.

But when she opened the door, her stomach fell. Of course, it wasn't Owen. Because if it had been, then her life would have been going down the path she wanted, the one she'd started to create.

Now, of course, it was careening off the edge of a cliff as she fought to hold on.

He didn't look much different. He was still the man who had walked out of her life all those years ago, away from the woman who hated her so much she'd tried to beat the life out of her countless times. His hair had gone grayer, but not that much. He'd put on a few pounds around his middle, but even that didn't look all that different. He still had those eyes that never saw her for who she could be, and that same smile that made her skin crawl because he just didn't *care*.

"What are you doing here?" she snapped. "How did you find out where I live?"

"Is that any way to greet your father?" the man who'd never bothered to raise her asked.

"Go away, old man. You walked away easily enough before. Just do it again." Her palms went clammy, and her stomach revolted.

"Now, Elizabeth. Please, listen to me. I'm here to make amends."

"You're about twenty years too late. Now get off my property before I call the cops."

"You wouldn't do that." Alarm crossed his features, and she didn't feel a damn thing about it.

"Yeah, I would. I'd call the cops like you should have done twenty years ago. Now get the fuck out of my life. You were just as bad as her, you know. You may not have hit me, but you let her do it. And I don't want an abuser in my life."

"I am *not* like her."

"Look in the mirror and see the neglectful abuser you are. I'm not the same little girl I once was who looked up to you and thought you could save me. You're nothing. Now go away."

And with that, she slammed the door in his face, her hands shaking. He'd brought everything back up again; everything that could destroy her soul, her life, her future. Bile filled her throat, and she pressed a hand to her stomach, over the life growing inside.

She couldn't become her mother.

She couldn't.

And she couldn't become her father...or allow Owen to be that man either.

She closed her eyes and sank to the floor, her body shaking. She had no idea what she was going to do, but she couldn't think about it now. *Tomorrow.* Tomorrow she'd find Owen and tell him what had happened. And the fact that she'd even thought of going to Owen for this told her one thing.

She was in love with him.

Now she just had to figure out what to do about it.

"Thanks, officer," Owen said into the phone. "Just let me know if you need anything else." He ended the call and stared blankly down at his hands. He couldn't quite believe what the officer had just told him, but the weight being lifted off his chest should have been enough.

"You okay?" Murphy asked as he walked into the office. "You're pale, man."

"That was the officer on my case. Apparently, they found the truck that hit me." And had basically left him for dead.

Murphy's eyes widened. "No shit?"

"No shit. Apparently, it was one of the drunk guys from the bar. The ones who were with Tessa. The ones I basically told to go screw themselves. He claims it was an accident because he was drunk driving and not because he was out to get me, but still. What the fuck, man?"

Murphy shook his head. "I hope he goes away for a long time for that. He could have killed you. Damn near did."

"I don't know what's going to happen or if there's even going to be a trial. I guess the police will let me know. But I suppose it's good that we know now, right? I mean, at least he's off the streets."

"I'd rather him have gotten off the streets before this if I'm honest."

"Well, that's true." Owen sank back into his chair and rubbed a hand over his face. "It's been an interesting couple of months."

"I'll say," Murphy added. "Well, I'd say let's go get a

drink tonight to celebrate, but that seems off, considering."

Owen snorted. "Yeah. Maybe a pizza or something. But not tonight since I promised Liz I'd help her with her plans."

Murphy saluted as he picked up the notebook he must have come into the office for. "And another one bites the dust."

Owen shrugged. "I'm really okay with that."

His brother smiled. "I'm glad, man. Seriously. I know I joke about how everyone is pairing off, but I'm happy about it."

"Are you going to settle down soon, then?" Owen asked.

"I have to live a little first, you know?" There was a seriousness in Murphy's eyes that hit Owen straight in the heart, but he didn't comment on it. It wasn't the time, and his brother wouldn't have wanted to hear it anyway. Instead, he nodded before watching Murphy walk out of the office, leaving Owen to his thoughts.

He'd been working his ass off filling the schedule after they'd lost that client. It still grated on him that the one thing he'd done by himself had failed, but his brothers had told him over and over again it wasn't his fault. Either way, though, Owen would make sure they filled the timeline and completed the best jobs they could.

The door opened once again, and he looked up, his brow lifting as Clive Roland stepped through the doorway.

"Owen, good. I found you."

Owen blinked before sitting back in his chair, not bothering to get up. He had no idea why this man was here after going with another company and doing it in poor fashion, and he had a bad feeling about why Roland was here now.

"What can I do for you, Clive?"

The older man rubbed his hands together and looked around Owen's office. He was onsite today, so they were in a trailer on the lot rather than his larger office in the building the Gallaghers owned. It wasn't much to look at since they didn't meet clients here, and from the way Clive shifted, the other man wasn't too impressed.

Too damn bad.

Owen had done all he could to sway the man, and the board had gone with cheaper labor in the end. Not his problem.

"Well, you see, the Roland Group is in a bit of a bind and could use your help."

Owen nodded, gesturing for the man to continue.

He wasn't surprised that they were in a bind, but he didn't know why this man was here now, asking for help.

"The company we hired is going back on a few promises that weren't laid out in the contract, and the city board isn't happy with the changes that are coming. They're actually *really* not happy. Plus, it looks like these guys are under investigation now for cutting corners on a previous project, and well...needless to say, the Group needs your help."

Owen shook his head. "I don't know what I can do for you, Clive. You turned us down, and we've already started filling the block we left for you."

"We can give you an incentive to drop them."

This man was a piece of work, for sure. And Owen was just now realizing how lucky they were that they *hadn't* gotten the job. While on paper, the Roland Group was first class, he could see that they'd gotten there by underhanded means that hadn't been whispered about anywhere Owen could find. And even though his brothers should have been here to help make this decision, Owen knew what his answer had to be. They'd trusted him before, and damn it, he'd earn that trust again.

"We can't do that."

"At least think about it."

"Clive—"

"What the hell is going on?" Liz asked from the doorway.

Owen stood up. "Liz?"

"Don't 'Liz' me," she snapped. "What are you doing here, Clive?"

Owen frowned as he moved toward her. "You know him?"

Liz snorted. "Like you didn't know."

"I've asked you to call me Dad, not Clive," the old man said shakily, and Owen froze.

She'd told him her father had a different last name, but never in his wildest dreams would Owen have thought Clive Roland was Liz's father. However, now that he looked at them, he saw that they had the same damn eyes. He swallowed hard, trying to get his bearings, but the look of betrayal on Liz's face rocked him to the core.

He'd made so much progress with what they had together, but he knew if he didn't say the right thing, *do* the right thing, he'd lose her forever.

"I didn't know," he croaked.

"How can I believe you?" she asked, her eyes wide. "How?"

Chapter Fourteen

Liz's heart thudded in her ears, and she did her best not to scream or run away right then. She couldn't quite believe what was happening.

"Now, honey, don't yell at this young man." Her father's words were sickly condescending, and she wanted to shake him. He was a hollow man who'd ignored her for most of her childhood, but if he ever did take the time to speak to her, he always used that voice.

She looked quickly over at Clive. "What did I say about getting near me? Get the fuck away."

"You need to go, Clive." Owen's voice was low, determined, as if he knew that everything was balancing on a knife's edge. She was right there with him, and yet she wasn't sure what she was going to say next once she opened her mouth.

"We weren't done talking business." Clive ran a hand through his hair, his eyes darting between them. "How do you know Liz?"

"Not your problem," Owen growled. "We're done with the Roland Group and you. Get out."

Her father—though she hesitated to call him that—looked between them once more before shuffling out, his head hanging. She honestly couldn't care about him right then. In fact, after last night, she'd decided to push him from her mind altogether. She'd wanted to think about the future, try to make sure she wasn't risking everything by falling for Owen, and yet the universe had smacked her in the face with its lies once more.

"Liz, talk to me," Owen said after a moment, his voice too calm, too practiced, as if he were afraid to make the wrong move and spook her. Well, too late, she was already spooked.

"Did you know?" she asked, her voice hollow. She couldn't meet his eyes, not then.

"Did I know that man was the bastard who hurt you? No. I had no idea. He had a different last name, and yeah, you mentioned that your mom changed your name to her maiden one after he left, but it never occurred to me that he could be that man. Never once."

She turned to him her body numb. "Never once?"

"No. I even talked to you about this guy. He's the client that dropped us."

She frowned. "Then why was he here?"

Owen ran a hand through his hair and scowled. "He said he made a mistake and wanted to hire us again."

The floor beneath her feet felt unsteady, and she reached out for the chair next to her to steady herself. She couldn't deal with the idea that that man would be working with Owen and the family who had said she could join them in any way she was willing. It didn't matter that it made no sense to the practical and logical part of her mind. It was the scared child part of her, the part that screamed and ranted and that no one had listened to. It was that part that made her eyes hurt and her brain not want to work quite right.

"You're going to work with him?"

Owen moved forward, but she took a step back. Once again, she caught the hurt look on his face, and she hated herself for it. She hated everything right then and didn't know what to do about it.

"You just heard me say we had no business to discuss."

"So you're not going to take the deal of a lifetime because of me, then?" Because she wasn't sure how she'd feel about that. He'd resent her for it later, and that's how the disease would spread, how the hatred within a relationship burned.

"Fuck, no. I'd already said no, but he didn't listen. Him being the prick who deserves to be shot for what he did to you just put the nail in the coffin." He moved closer, and this time, she didn't back away. He cupped her face, but she didn't lean into him. "I love you, Lizzie. I'm not going to let that man and everything he's done hurt us."

She blinked, tears finally falling from her eyes. All of the emotions she'd buried for so long came to the surface, and she couldn't quite catch her breath.

"But what if he already has?"

"We can't let him. He's gone, Lizzie. He's gone." He pleaded with her, but some small part of her still rebelled, still worried that things could go wrong and everyone would be hurt worse in the process. Her father showing up here had to be a sign, and it was one she needed to pay attention to.

Only she couldn't think with Owen touching her, and she couldn't push through the worries and logic that came with everything they'd gone through up until now.

"I came here to tell you I got a job offer," she blurted. "It's in Cheyenne."

He stiffened, his hands falling from her face. "Cheyenne is a hell of a commute, Lizzie."

"I'd have to move there," she said hoarsely. "But it would be a position higher than the one I had, with better pay and hours."

"And you'd take it? Just like that?"

She was hurting him, and she didn't know how to stop it. She hadn't planned to take the damn job at all, but she didn't say that. She just kept rambling about benefits and everything that came with the position she didn't want. But her father had just been in that damn room, reminding her of everything she could become if she fell in love with Owen.

Only she knew it was too late.

She already loved him.

And now she had to get some space so she wouldn't break him.

"I don't know yet, but I need to know my options."

"*I'm* your option, Lizzie. You, me, and the baby. You can't just leave because you're scared."

"I don't know what I'm doing!" she yelled and wrapped her arms around her waist. "Ever since I met you, everything I've built feels like it's falling apart around me. I thought I was so strong, so independent, but instead, I keep freaking out and crying and saying the wrong things. I don't like this person, Owen. I don't like who I'm becoming."

"It's because you're fighting it. If you'd just let yourself fall, you wouldn't hate yourself." His eyes pleaded with her, but all she could think of was him hating her for what she could do if she weren't careful.

She didn't want to leave. Didn't want to *not* love him.

But she was so *scared*.

"I don't know how to fall," she whispered. "And I need to make sure I don't hurt our baby because I'm making the wrong choices. Can't you just give me time to process all of this?"

Owen put his hands on his hips, his eyes dark and full of pain as he studied her face. She wanted to reach out to him, but she was afraid she would do something stupid. She'd known her whole life that if she fell for a man and let him change her, she'd become the one thing she hated. And to be with Owen, she'd have to push through that. She'd thought she'd started to, but having her father shoved back in her face only made it that much harder.

"I love you, Lizzie. With everything I have. I'll give you time to think, but I'm not going anywhere. You know what I feel, what I want. But I can't force you to love me. I can't force you to stay."

She reached out for him, but let her hand fall.

She couldn't touch him and think; couldn't touch him and remember why she was fighting this.

So she turned on her heel and left, knowing she was probably making the worst decision of her life. This was for Owen. And she knew that for the lie it was. But if she left now, she could think and could make sure she didn't hurt him.

Tears slid down her cheeks as she ran to her car, ignoring the shouts from Graham and Murphy as they called out to her. She couldn't face them. Not with what she'd just done.

Instead, she drove home, her attention on the road and nothing else. She couldn't formulate thoughts beyond the pounding in her head that screamed at her to turn back. By the time she pulled into her driveway and stumbled through her front door, she knew she'd made a horrible mistake.

She was *not* her mother.

She was *not* her father.

So they'd fucked each other over as well as her, but she was *not* them. She didn't want the damn job in Cheyenne and knew there was that business card on her dresser calling out to her. She would have to change the way she'd done her job for years to make it happen, but she could. Just as she'd begun to change the way she thought about life in general. She shouldn't have left Owen. Hell, she was going fucking crazy. Of course, he didn't know, but she had just been looking for an excuse to mess everything up as always. She'd done the one thing she'd promise not to do: hurt him.

She had to find him. Had to go back.

Liz pressed her hand over her belly and took a deep breath. She had to do what she'd sworn she would never do and admit to falling completely and madly in love with Owen Gallagher, taking the risk of a lifetime along the way.

Decision made, she let out a breath. She'd been scared and had acted rashly, something she'd never done, at least not until she was knocked off her feet the first time she met Owen. He'd been right—if she hadn't fought as hard as she was, she wouldn't have reacted the way she had so many times.

Maybe once she admitted to him that she loved him, that she wanted him, that she trusted him, she wouldn't continue down the path of turning into a person she hardly recognized.

At least she hoped.

As she turned to pick up the keys that had fallen to the floor without her noticing, the doorbell rang. She froze. Before she could look through the peephole to see who it was, a deep voice on the other side of the door told her.

"Open the damn door, Lizzie. We're not done."

No, they weren't. Not by a long shot.

She took a deep breath and stepped into her fate as she opened the door.

Liz stood in front of him as she opened the door, her face pale, her cheeks stained with tears, but she had opened the damn door. That had to count for something.

"Owen."

"Are you going to let me in, or are we going to let the rest of the neighborhood hear what I have to say?" He was so damn mad right then, he couldn't think straight, but he knew it wasn't completely her fault. Things kept getting in their way, but he'd be damned if he let that stop them from getting everything they deserved.

Liz was the best thing that had ever happened to him, and she needed to know that.

And hell, he hoped he was the best damn thing that had happened to her, as well.

She quickly moved out of the way, and he stomped inside, grateful when she closed the door behind him.

"I shouldn't have let you leave like that," he started. "You were upset, and yet I just let you get in your car and drive off. Who knows what could have happened? I mean, fuck, they caught the guy that hit me, but there are countless others."

Her eyes widened, and she took a step toward him. "They found him?"

Hell, he'd almost forgotten all about it. It seemed like ages ago that he'd gotten the news, not merely an hour. "Yeah. It was one of the guys from the bar that had too much to drink. He didn't even realize he hit me he was so far gone."

She let out a breath. "I'm glad they caught him, but I still want to kick him in the nuts for hurting you."

He let out a rough chuckle. "Yeah, I kind of do, too." He blew out a breath, running his hands through his hair. He'd never used to do that as often as he did now, but Liz kept stressing him out, setting off nervous ticks.

"I was careful driving," she said softly. "I kept my attention on the road and would have pulled over if it was too much. I was an idiot, but not reckless with my life or our child's life. I promise."

He closed his eyes, trying to calm himself. "You're not an idiot, Liz."

"Yeah, I kind of am. I keep running away when I get scared, and that only ends up hurting both of us."

His eyes shot open as her words penetrated. "What are you saying?"

She moved forward, pressing her hands to his chest. "I shouldn't have left when I did. How I did."

"Damn right." He cupped her face. "You're everything to me. You and the baby. Which, can I add how fucking nervous I am that we're having a baby? Because, hell, I still can't believe this is happening, but I know we can do this because we'll do it together."

She pressed her lips together and blinked. "It doesn't feel real. We keep saying the word and yet..."

"I know, Lizzie. I know. It's all been go, go, go since we started out, and we're still getting used to the idea of us. But, Liz? I'm not letting you run away again. I'll just keep following because you only run when you're scared, not because you don't want to be near me." He winced. "Okay, that sounds like I'm a stalker, but I'm trying to be romantic. There's a thin line."

She raised a brow. "Not as thin as you think, but I know what you mean." She met his gaze and rolled her shoulders back as if preparing to say something she wasn't sure she was ready for. "I love you, Owen."

His heart pounded at the words, and it took everything within him not to react and pull her close. He wanted to taste her lips, know how she felt against him now that they had both finally told each other the truth of what they felt.

"I have for a while now, but I just couldn't see it. Or

maybe I could and that's why I kept holding myself back. Every time I felt like I was almost there or at least close enough that I could trust myself, something else happened. Between the pregnancy, my job, and then my father of all people, it was all so much."

He brushed his thumb along her jaw. "But you handled it."

She snorted. "Not well."

He couldn't correct her there. "We all handle things differently, and yeah, you were overwhelmed, but I wasn't much better. I started making lists and trying to take care of things on my own without asking for help. It roped me off from everyone, including you, and I shouldn't have done that."

"I'm not going to Cheyenne," she blurted. "I never was, but apparently, I needed an out, so when things got to be too much, I used it."

"Damn right, you weren't going to Cheyenne." He paused, thoughtful. "Of course, Gallagher Brothers Restoration could always use a satellite office up there just in case." He rubbed his chin. "Not a bad idea, actually."

She rolled her eyes and punched at him. "Stop it. I'm not going."

"But if you did, I'd go with you. I love you, Liz.

You're my future, don't you get that? Where you go, I go."

Tears filled her eyes, and he was afraid he'd said the wrong thing until she kissed the center of his chest. "I'm going to make mistakes, Owen. I'm going to do something rash and stupid when I'm upset, even if I'm trying to do the right thing. I'm probably going to be overwhelmed with finding a new job and being pregnant, not to mention the whole part that happens after raising a baby. And I want to be with you, I do, but I can't just leave Tessa on her own in this house we bought, so I'm probably going to stress out about that too and cause you to stress, as well. I'm just laying it out there. I love you, but I come with a lot of baggage."

Owen tucked her close, not quite ready to believe that everything he'd ever wanted could be in his arms right then. Holy hell, he never truly thought this could happen, and yet he knew it was.

Liz was *his*.

Finally.

"We all have baggage, Lizzie." She snorted. "Some more than others, sure, but we all have it. Hell, you're going to have to deal with my organizational tendencies and the fact that I tend to over plan things. Daily."

"Still not as much baggage as me," she muttered into his chest.

"Well, it's not a competition, and I'm sure you'll find things that annoy you about me over time. But that's the thing, Lizzie, it's *time*. I want you by my side and in my life until the day we move on to the next. I want to raise our child together and make mistakes, knowing we can fix them if we try. And if you get scared, promise not to run. Because if you do, I'll just hold you captive with paperclips and binder clips if I have to. I have a desk full of them."

She blinked at him for a moment before throwing her head back and laughing. "You're such a dork, Owen Gallagher."

He sobered before gently pressing a kiss to her sweet, sweet lips. "I'm your dork, Lizzie. All you have to do is stay."

She looked into his eyes, and they both let out a soft breath. "I'll stay. As long as you're here, I'll stay."

Owen's heart threatened to explode as he took her mouth again in a heated kiss. He had his woman, the one who would test him and keep him on his toes until the end of his days, and soon, he'd have a new life to nurture and teach how to plan things when everything got to be too much.

And when he couldn't quite take it all, he knew he wouldn't be alone.

Because the woman in jeans who'd knocked his

socks off the first night he'd met her had overcome everything inside her and in her past so she could be his as much as he could be hers.

There were no lists or spreadsheets for that kind of destiny and chance.

And that, Owen Gallagher knew, was just fine with him.

THE END

Coming Next: Murphy and Tessa Change the Rules in <u>Hope Restored</u>

IF YOU'D LIKE TO READ A BONUS SCENE FROM
PASSION RESTORED:
CHECK OUT THIS SPECIAL EPILOGUE!

A Note from Carrie Ann

Thank you so much for reading **PASSION RESTORED**. The Gallagher Brothers series is a spin off of the Montgomery Ink series and I'm so happy to keep expanding that world. If you haven't picked up the Montgomerys, DELICATE INK is the first book in the series.

Next up in the Gallagher Brothers is <u>Hope Restored</u>. Murphy and Tessa have been teasing me for awhile and I know their story is going to be a hard one...I can't wait for you guys to check it out.

Thank you so much for reading and I hope you loved the Gallagher Brothers!

The Gallagher Brothers Series:

Book 1: <u>Love Restored</u>

Book 2: <u>Passion Restored</u>

Book 3: <u>Hope Restored</u>

If you want to make sure you know what's coming next from me, you can sign up for my newsletter at www. CarrieAnnRyan.com; follow me on twitter at @CarrieAnnRyan, or like my Facebook page. I also have a Facebook Fan Club where we have trivia, chats, and other goodies. You guys are the reason I get to do what I do and I thank you.

Make sure you're signed up for my MAILING LIST so you can know when the next releases are available as well as find giveaways and FREE READS.

Happy Reading!

Also from Carrie Ann Ryan

The Montgomery Ink Legacy Series:

Book 1: Bittersweet Promises (Leif & Brooke)

Book 2: At First Meet (Nick & Lake)

Book 2.5: Happily Ever Never (May & Leo)

Book 3: Longtime Crush (Sebastian & Raven)

Book 4: Best Friend Temptation (Noah, Ford, and Greer)

Book 4.5: Happily Ever Maybe (Jennifer & Gus)

Book 5: Last First Kiss (Daisy & Hugh)

Book 6: His Second Chance (Kane & Phoebe)

Book 7: One Night with You (Kingston & Claire)

The Wilder Brothers Series:

Book 1: One Way Back to Me (Eli & Alexis)

Book 2: Always the One for Me (Evan & Kendall)

Book 3: The Path to You (Everett & Bethany)

Book 4: Coming Home for Us (Elijah & Maddie)

Book 5: Stay Here With Me (East & Lark)

Book 6: Finding the Road to Us (Elliot, Trace, and Sidney)

Book 7: Moments for You (Ridge & Aurora)

Book 7.5: A Wilder Wedding (Amos & Naomi)

Book 8: Forever For Us (Wyatt & Ava)

The Cage Family

Book 1: The Forever Rule (Aston & Emma)

The First Time Series:

Book 1: Good Time Boyfriend (Heath & Denver)

Book 2: Last Minute Fiancé (Luca & Addison)

Book 3: Second Chance Husband (August & Paisley)

The Montgomery Ink: Fort Collins Series:

Book 1: Inked Persuasion (Jacob & Annabelle)

Book 2: Inked Obsession (Beckett & Eliza)

Book 3: Inked Devotion (Benjamin & Brenna)

Book 3.5: Nothing But Ink (Clay & Riggs)

Book 4: Inked Craving (Lee & Paige)

Book 5: Inked Temptation (Archer & Killian)

The Montgomery Ink: Boulder Series:

Book 1: Wrapped in Ink (Liam & Arden)

Book 2: Sated in Ink (Ethan, Lincoln, and Holland)

Book 3: Embraced in Ink (Bristol & Marcus)

Book 3: Moments in Ink (Zia & Meredith)

Book 4: Seduced in Ink (Aaron & Madison)

Book 4.5: Captured in Ink (Julia, Ronin, & Kincaid)

Book 4.7: Inked Fantasy (Secret ??)

Book 4.8: A Very Montgomery Christmas (The Entire Boulder Family)

Montgomery Ink: Colorado Springs

Book 1: Fallen Ink (Adrienne & Mace)

Book 2: Restless Ink (Thea & Dimitri)

Book 2.5: Ashes to Ink (Abby & Ryan)

Book 3: Jagged Ink (Roxie & Carter)

Book 3.5: Ink by Numbers (Landon & Kaylee)

Montgomery Ink Denver:

Book 0.5: Ink Inspired (Shep & Shea)

Book 0.6: Ink Reunited (Sassy, Rare, and Ian)

Book 1: Delicate Ink (Austin & Sierra)

Book 1.5: Forever Ink (Callie & Morgan)

Book 2: Tempting Boundaries (Decker and Miranda)

Book 3: Harder than Words (Meghan & Luc)

Book 3.5: Finally Found You (Mason & Presley)

Book 4: Written in Ink (Griffin & Autumn)

Book 4.5: Hidden Ink (Hailey & Sloane)

Book 5: Ink Enduring (Maya, Jake, and Border)

Book 6: Ink Exposed (Alex & Tabby)

Book 6.5: Adoring Ink (Holly & Brody)

Book 6.6: Love, Honor, & Ink (Arianna & Harper)

Book 7: Inked Expressions (Storm & Everly)

Book 7.3: Dropout (Grayson & Kate)

Book 7.5: Executive Ink (Jax & Ashlynn)

Book 8: Inked Memories (Wes & Jillian)

Book 8.5: Inked Nights (Derek & Olivia)

Book 8.7: Second Chance Ink (Brandon & Lauren)

Book 8.5: Montgomery Midnight Kisses (Alex & Tabby Bonus(

Bonus: Inked Kingdom (Stone & Sarina)

The On My Own Series:

Book 0.5: My First Glance

Book 1: My One Night (Dillon & Elise)

Book 2: My Rebound (Pacey & Mackenzie)

Book 3: My Next Play (Miles & Nessa)

Book 4: My Bad Decisions (Tanner & Natalie)

The Promise Me Series:

Book 1: Forever Only Once (Cross & Hazel)

Book 2: From That Moment (Prior & Paris)

Book 3: Far From Destined (Macon & Dakota)

Book 4: From Our First (Nate & Myra)

The Less Than Series:

Book 1: Breathless With Her (Devin & Erin)

Book 2: Reckless With You (Tucker & Amelia)

Book 3: Shameless With Him (Caleb & Zoey)

The Fractured Connections Series:

Book 1: Breaking Without You (Cameron & Violet)

Book 2: Shouldn't Have You (Brendon & Harmony)

Book 3: Falling With You (Aiden & Sienna)

Book 4: Taken With You (Beckham & Meadow)

The Whiskey and Lies Series:

Book 1: Whiskey Secrets (Dare & Kenzie)

Book 2: Whiskey Reveals (Fox & Melody)

Book 3: Whiskey Undone (Loch & Ainsley)

The Gallagher Brothers Series:

Book 1: Love Restored (Graham & Blake)

Book 2: Passion Restored (Owen & Liz)

Book 3: Hope Restored (Murphy & Tessa)

The Ravenwood Coven Series:

Book 1: Dawn Unearthed

Book 2: Dusk Unveiled

Book 3: Evernight Unleashed

The Aspen Pack Series:

Book 1: Etched in Honor

Book 2: Hunted in Darkness

Book 3: Mated in Chaos

Book 4: Harbored in Silence

Book 5: Marked in Flames

The Talon Pack:

Book 1: Tattered Loyalties

Book 2: An Alpha's Choice

Book 3: Mated in Mist

Book 4: Wolf Betrayed

Book 5: Fractured Silence

Book 6: Destiny Disgraced

Book 7: Eternal Mourning

Book 8: Strength Enduring

Book 9: Forever Broken

Book 10: Mated in Darkness

Book 11: Fated in Winter

Redwood Pack Series:

Book 1: An Alpha's Path

Book 2: <u>A Taste for a Mate</u>

Book 3: <u>Trinity Bound</u>

Book 3.5: <u>A Night Away</u>

Book 4: <u>Enforcer's Redemption</u>

Book 4.5: <u>Blurred Expectations</u>

Book 4.7: <u>Forgiveness</u>

Book 5: <u>Shattered Emotions</u>

Book 6: <u>Hidden Destiny</u>

Book 6.5: <u>A Beta's Haven</u>

Book 7: <u>Fighting Fate</u>

Book 7.5: <u>Loving the Omega</u>

Book 7.7: <u>The Hunted Heart</u>

Book 8: <u>Wicked Wolf</u>

The Elements of Five Series:

Book 1: From Breath and Ruin

Book 2: From Flame and Ash

Book 3: From Spirit and Binding

Book 4: From Shadow and Silence

Dante's Circle Series:

Book 1: <u>Dust of My Wings</u>

Book 2: <u>Her Warriors' Three Wishes</u>

Book 3: <u>An Unlucky Moon</u>

Book 3.5: <u>His Choice</u>

Book 4: <u>Tangled Innocence</u>

Book 5: <u>Fierce Enchantment</u>

Book 6: <u>An Immortal's Song</u>

Book 7: <u>Prowled Darkness</u>

Book 8: Dante's Circle Reborn

Holiday, Montana Series:

Book 1: <u>Charmed Spirits</u>

Book 2: <u>Santa's Executive</u>

Book 3: <u>Finding Abigail</u>

Book 4: <u>Her Lucky Love</u>

Book 5: Dreams of Ivory

The Branded Pack Series:
(Written with Alexandra Ivy)

Book 1: <u>Stolen and Forgiven</u>

Book 2: <u>Abandoned and Unseen</u>

Book 3: <u>Buried and Shadowed</u>

About the Author

Carrie Ann Ryan is the New York Times and USA Today bestselling author of contemporary, paranormal, and young adult romance. Her works include the Montgomery Ink, Redwood Pack, Fractured Connections, and Elements of Five series, which have sold over 3.0 million books worldwide. She started writing while in graduate school for her advanced degree in chemistry and hasn't stopped since. Carrie Ann has written over seventy-five novels and novellas with more in the works. When she's not losing herself in her emotional and action-packed worlds, she's reading as much as she can while wrangling her clowder of cats who have more followers than she does.

www.CarrieAnnRyan.com